T0123504

books by *Barbara G Louise*
published by iUniverse (if I live long enough)

[7)]A Unicorn of KKhadee
[1)]The Invasion of Peasant-Earth
[2)]The Milky Galaxy
[8)]The Gay Gift

<u>the rabble and the Rich series:</u>
(the story in each book is complete and can stand alone)

[3)]The Butterfly Caper
[4)]The Secret Experiment
[5)]Learning to Share
[6)]Inherit the Earth

THE
MILKY
GALAXY

iUniverse®

THE MILKY GALAXY

iUniverse books may be ordered through booksellers or by contacting:

iUniverse
1663 Liberty Drive
Bloomington, IN 47403
www.iuniverse.com
844-349-9409

Because of the dynamic nature of the Internet, any web addresses or links contained in this book may have changed since publication and may no longer be valid. The views expressed in this work are solely those of the author and do not necessarily reflect the views of the publisher, and the publisher hereby disclaims any responsibility for them.

Any people depicted in stock imagery provided by Getty Images are models, and such images are being used for illustrative purposes only. Certain stock imagery © Getty Images.

ISBN: 978-1-6632-3178-9 (sc)
ISBN: 978-1-6632-3179-6 (e)

Library of Congress Control Number: 2021923048

Print information available on the last page.

iUniverse rev. date: 01/21/2022

in memory of my beloved father,

James Born Whittum
who introduced me to science fiction

"Never underestimate the power of fiction to tell the truth."

~ Leslie Feinberg
commentary on <u>Stone Butch Blues</u>

introduction

Once upon a time, twenty billion years ago, in a mediocre galaxy which later grew to become the Milky, on an ordinary, rocky planet orbiting a great blue-white star — in the warm, sweet, salty ocean which covered that planet — a chance combination of organic molecules were struck by an extremely energetic cosmic ray from the blue-white sun, and Lo! Life began!

Some would say, *God* had a hand in it: the first creation of Life in that galaxy. Many species would later arise in the Milky Galaxy and praise *Chance* — or (*readers choice*), *the-One-and-only-God, or a collection of deities* — for the benevolent creation of the amiable Geejjikk.

Those Geejjikk — green in colour, because of an analog to chlorophyll — were capable of independent, energetic, protein-based motility — (combining the attributes of both plants and animals) — and were the first species to achieve sapience in the Milky Galaxy. They went on to create the first, and only — *Way-of-the-Milk (*nurturing) Galactic Civilization — sharing their goodwill, and brilliant scientific discoveries, with all other sapient species as each arose from — and finally *rejected* — the *vicious competitiveness* of their early, pre-Space development.

At first in that "warm, sweet, salty ocean," the first cell, ecstatic — (*if a single cell could be said to have any emotion at all)* — ecstatic with the joy of suddenly being alive! — had chaotically divided and divided, forming many daughter cells. Then those first cells had combined to form a unique multi-cellular animal, unlike any that had ever appeared in that galaxy, or ever would.

In the usual development of multi-cellular organisms, all the DNA of the animal's (or plant's) genome is found in each and every cell of the organism. Nevertheless, usually, the body of each animal or plant differentiates into various distinct organs to perform specific tasks, like pumping fluids, sensing the environment (light, sound, temperature, etc.), communicating with others, absorbing food and water, and so forth.

Differently, in the Geejjikk — in every cell of the being's amorphous, DNA body — each cell retained its potential and its individuality, and was capable of altering its shape and its biochemistry to perform any task necessary for the life of the multi-cellular organism. This was unique, and remained so among other sapient creatures in that odd corner of the infinite Multiverse.

The Geejjikk looked like giant amoebas, and as green blobs, because of their extremely pleasant personalties — and their irrepressibly generous spirit — they became the most beloved sapient species of all in that galaxy they came to call the Milky.

book one
THE RUINED EARTH

*   *   *

Eeelk was the only alien on Earth.

At first, Eeelk had avoided the Humans, who like hirself had been left behind when the vast ships of the Geejjikk had lifted off and had fled — gravid with volunteer Humans and the plants and animals needed to sustain them — into interstellar space, headed for the wormhole in the Alpha Centauri star-system. Eeelk had known zee would look like a large, amoeboid, amorphous, green blob to the people of Earth, although zee was a multi-cellular being, each of whose cells could fulfill any function, from taste, sight, and hearing to absorption of nutrients or detailed chemical analysis of potential poisons.

Eeelk's species had only one gender. When referring to Eeelk in English, there was no use for 'he' or 'she,' just the one neutral pronoun: 'zee,' and only one other pronoun for a unisexual being: 'hir,' instead of 'him,' 'her,' 'his,' or 'hers.'

Animal life on Earth was mostly of the small insectoid flying or crawling variety, whose short individual life spans and quick breeding cycles had enabled the tiny animals to evolve into new species which were extremely resistant to the foul air, poisoned soil, and filthy water of their dying planet.

At any time, with the casual swoop of an extruded pseudopod through the air, Eeelk could capture many of the small flying things as an easy snack. Eeelk had to absorb protein, fat, and carbohydrates, like any animal, for energy and for physical bulk. (Hir green colour, pseudo-chlorophyll, did not absorb enough energy from the sun to animate hir large animal body.)

Until zee was accidentally abandoned, Eeelk had been part of an integrated Galactic culture, wherein many different sapient species lived together and enjoyed sharing each other's cultures and unique world-views.

Eeelk, like all members of hir species, could eat almost anything, by absorbing it directly into hir body. Even though the plants zee ate were greatly mutated from what had once been their healthy, stable forms, food was not a problem.

The only earth-animals which were large enough to be truly 'meaty' — and therefore substantial enough to be a complete-protein-meal — were also hunted by the Humans. Eeelk shied away from directly competing with the Humans for food, since the indigenous sapient species of Earth was obviously on the edge of extinction. The Humans were struggling hard to survive in their ruined environment, but there were plenty of the meat-creatures — called 'rats' and 'rabbits' by the Humans — to go around. . . .

Unfortunately, the urge to *communicate* had settled over Eeelk several days after zee had been abandoned. Eeelk missed sharing memories with hir siblings. The loss was painful. The *Four* would have conversed together during their first year after birth their entire childhoods, sharing and reinforcing those memories each had inherited from hir parents. Eeelk and hir three siblings had been created from mixing and re-combining the genetic material of their parents — two of them, although their species had only one gender. The parents had disappeared in the Reproductive Act, each giving up hir individual existence in the total genetic merging of their bodies and in the ecstatic fusion-and-fission creation of their *Four* children.

Each small child – about half the size of one of the parents – carried some of the memories of hir parents as well as hir own unique combination of their genetic material. Waves of sadness washed through hir amorphous body as Eeelk remembered the warmth of their childhood nest, the *Four* communicating together constantly, reinforcing the memories they shared which stretched back to the beginning of their species' collective existence. Maintenance of racial memory was of critical importance to each member of Eeelk's species.

Heedless of the impending departure of so many sapients from Earth, Eeelk had gone exploring and had only known hirself abandoned when zee saw the propulsion trails of the great starships above hir in the grimy sky of Earth. Since then, Eeelk had been alone and deeply concerned about hir isolation. Food was not a problem, so all of hir time could be spent worrying about how hir memories — the priceless and only legacy Eeelk could give to hir species — could be passed on to future generations, since there was seemingly no other Geejjikk on Earth for Eeelk to mate with and produce another *Four*.

Hir thoughts were interrupted by the sudden appearance of two groups of Humans.

"Ssst! A Guard! Over there," one of the young Human Hunters urgently whispered, touching a smaller Hunter on the shoulder and pointing at a heavily-armed Guard.

The Guard and its two identically-armored companions moved through a landscape of ruined city buildings, crumbling wrecks bristling with jagged I-beams, smoke-damaged piles of old brick, and a wilderness of broken windows. The only buildings to survive intact had apparently been tightly boarded-up some time before in a more prudent past.

Cocked and loaded crossbow in hand, the smaller Hunter studied the guards, employees of the 'Boogees,' Rich people, the Bourgeoisie, who lived in five-mile-high Domes where they selfishly preserved clean air, water, and good food for themselves, locking-out all members of the former working class.

The young lookout had just warned the rest of the party of their near presence. Three armed Human Guards wearing modern, flexible, metal-and-dense-plastic-composite armor were walking brazenly down the street of the former Cleveland inner-city neighborhood. They walked bareheaded, without the helmets sealed to their body armor, using only mouth-and-nose masks for protection from the foul air. Their arrogant openness advertised their contempt for any dangers the dirty ruined 'slums' might pose for them.

An ugly, gray, boxy bot-cleaner rolled before them, pushing trash and debris out of their way. Watching from cover, the Hunters saw the robot clear a path through the rotted boards of a collapsed Victorian porch *right outside a window leading into the sealed buildings where Eeelk knew the Humans lived in hiding!*

A Guard used the butt of hir automatic rifle to break a blackened glass window, partially dislodging the wooden insert sealing the window. Quickly, the smaller Hunter raised its weapon to a padded shoulder and — barely touching the daVinci-design hair-trigger of the crossbow — with an easy flick of a trigger finger, skewered the Guard through hir neck with a steel bolt tipped with a four-sided quarrel. The Guard was dead before zee could completely dislodge the wooden insert and climb into the clean, lived-in bedroom with its door leading into the rest of the hidden Community.

The smaller Hunter who had fired the crossbow whispered hoarsely to the others: "Let's move!

"Give me your bow," the smaller Hunter hissed to someone else once they had changed positions. "Take mine."

Fifty feet further on, the smaller Hunter stood up from cover and aimed at another Guard, above hir shoulders, where zee foolishly wasn't armored. The Guard pointed and cried out, seeing the Hunter in an instant before the crossbow bolt entered hir eye and brain.

"Down!" the Hunter hissed to hir companions.

The community hunting party flattened themselves to the ground behind a tall petrified pile of trash in time to avoid automatic-weapon's fire from the last living Guard.

A few minutes and many thousands of rounds later, apparently convinced nothing could have survived its bullets, the Guard slung hir automatic rifle over hir shoulder, turned toward the scene of the first death on the collapsed Victorian porch, and reached for hir radio to inform its base of the situation.

Someone handed the smaller Hunter another crossbow, already re-armed and re-cocked. The last Guard could not be allowed to radio knowledge of the crossbow-armed Hunters and the clean, intact room behind the broken window. The survival of the hidden Human Community rested on their remaining unknown to the greedy Boogees, the rich and powerful Humans Eeelk knew lived nearby under five-mile-high geodesic domes with a clean water and air supply, and uncontaminated food.

The small Hunter shot the last Boogee-Guard through the back of hir neck, and through the wrist of the hand which held the radio up to hir mouth. An incoherent gurgle was all the radio-listener could have heard.

Crossbows at the ready, the Hunters watched for other Guards who might be in the area, while one Hunter with a talent for speed and invisibility retrieved their crossbow bolts from the bodies of the three dead Guards. Then, emboldened by the apparent lack of other Guards in the area, the Hunters dragged the dead Guard off the ruined front porch of the Victorian house, and left him to be eaten by rats with the other two Guards on the decades-high piles of petrified trash and rotten garbage blocking the former city sidewalks. The hunting party retrieved three automatic rifles, clips of ammunition, and the radio. Those Hunters who were not wounded rushed to relieve the fresh corpses of their clothing and their armor. Footprints in the snow were carefully wiped away. They left no easily discernible trace of the battle and who had fought it. They had 'killed' the cleaner-bot also, so they could take it back with them to strip for parts.

Eeelk watched with admiration as the Hunters, finished with scavenging the dead guards, quickly returned to the relative safety of their sealed Community. One Hunter helped another who had gotten a bullet crease across the back of hir head, and two others helped another who had taken a bullet through hir heel, perhaps crippling hir for life.

Then the Geejjikk returned to hir own hunt for food.

*   *   *

A few days later, Eeelk had been watching one rat for a long time. Zee was again close to some Human habitations, but hidden in the wreckage of a collapsed building. No Human seemed to be stalking that particular rat, which was itself engaged in hunting smaller prey, a mouse. It was aware of Eeelk, but only as part of the inanimate background environment. It was not aware the alien was alive because Eeelk did not smell like a familiar animal of Earth. Everything living in its world was to the rat either prey to kill and eat, or a predator to fear.

Eeelk was just beginning to contemplate snaring the rat with a pseudopod, when zee sensed the approach of a Human Hunter.

Cocked and loaded crossbow in hand, the small Hunter Eeelk recognized from the battle with the Boogee-guards smiled when she saw the rat. Eeelk could see – since zee was close to the Human – she was obviously of the woman gender. She was less than five *gessk* tall, with light brown skin, curly white hair, and apparently most of her own teeth. She wore thick-glass, rubber-rimmed corrective-goggles tied tightly on her head with a piece of recycled cotton cord, and a plastic breathing mask over her mouth and nose, with tubing running to the compressed-air tank on her back. The exposed skin of her face was shiny with a yellowish-paste of insect-repellant. She wore long-pants tucked into high boots and a long-sleeved shirt with rubber bands sealing it at the wrists to soft leather gloves. Zee could see the woman had ample mammary-glands on her chest beneath her shirt.

The rat was busy being a predator, forgetting it could also be prey. The woman raised the crossbow to her padded shoulder and looked through her telescopic sight at the rat pausing in front of Eeelk, who was posing as a large green, free-standing plastic-wall. *Must have been left over*, the woman thought, *from an earlier age. Why haven't I seen it before?*

Eeelk was a youngling who had not yet developed hir full adult powers of restraint to match the strong ethical sense zee had inherited. Despite the presence of the Human, zee lashed out hungrily with a pseudopod and engulfed the rat.

At that same instant, barely touching the daVinci-design hair-trigger of her crossbow, the woman skewered the rat with a steel bolt tipped with a four-sided quarrel. She was obviously a good shot. To her, the dead rat suddenly appeared to be covered with a blob of dark green plastic. The bolt had gone through the green stuff to kill the rat.

The small Hunter saw a shiny green trumpet-mouth extrude itself from the 'wall of old green plastic.' She stiffened with surprise when the *'plastic'* trumpet said, "Please do not be alarmed. I know I look like a giant amoeba, but I am a Sapient Being like yourself."

The Human sat down suddenly on the remains of an old brick sitting-wall, and said, "Oh; a Geejjikk."

"Yes, I am a Geejjikk. You can have the rat. Retrieve your bolt and I will extrude the rat, unless . . . perhaps? You might want me to take off the fur? Which I understand you Humans cannot eat."

"Uh . . ." (The Human needed time to grasp the enormous change in her situation.) "No, umm . . . leave the fur," she said. We need the pelt, but . . . could you do something else for me?"

"Sure," Eeelk said through the trumpet, surprising the small Human with hir use of colloquial English.

"Oh!" (She took a deep breath and concentrated on creating the alpha waves necessary to slow her heart rate.) "Living in the fur of the rat, there will probably be small insects we call fleas, which might be carrying a terrible disease we call Plague. Unless the disease will hurt you, could you please eat all the fleas?"

"The disease won't hurt me at all. I have eaten all the fleas. They were a small tasty snack. You may have the rat now." The green 'plastic' flowed away from the dead rat.

Apparently believing the Geejjikk about the fleas, and keeping her eye on the trumpet, the woman went forward and picked up the dead rat by its naked tail, retrieving her crossbow bolt. Then she addressed the trumpet sticking out from the green wall, "My name is Ruth Green. Do you have a name?"

"Yes. Eeelk, child of Speet-&-Eeesk."

"Nice to meet you, Eeelk."

"Nice to meet you, Ruthgreen. I am glad my form does not frighten or disgust you."

"Of course not." Ruth refrained from telling the alien she actually thought he (no! – *zee!*) was *kind of cute, in an adorable green-blob sort of way.* . . . "Uh, why are you still here on Earth?" she asked.

"It was a mistake. I wandered off. I am very young."

"Oh, I'm so sorry."

"Sorry I am young?"

"No, no, no. Sorry you were left here on Earth by mistake. You must miss your family. Do you Geejjikk have families?" The woman put the dead rat into a canvas bag and slung it over her shoulder.

"I miss talking to my siblings, sharing our parental memories," Eeelk answered.

"Why don't you come along with me then? You could join our Community. I'm sure lots of people would enjoy talking to you," she said.

"But you are the Humans who refused to go out into space with my people. We thought you didn't like aliens."

"Not true. Those of us who elected to stay on the planet of our birth did so for many reasons not having anything to do with you Geejjikk, or what you look like. Really."

"Oh. Well, okay."

Ruth decided one rat and one interesting green amoeboid-alien were enough to bring back from an afternoon's solo hunting trip. She led Eeelk — who slithered quietly behind her — to the 'Hunter's Gate', the nearest airlock into the local sealed Human buildings. Her palm print and a password caused a begrimed '*concrete*' wall to scrape noisily aside and reveal Ruth's Community's largest airlock. She entered, turned and watched with delight as Eeelk, green and amorphous, squeaked into the airlock. Zee elongated hir form until zee rose seven feet tall, two feet over the small Human's head, to touch the ceiling.

Ruth pulled a large plastic bag off a clip on the wall of the airlock and put her weapons, breathing mask, and oxy-nitrogen tanks inside the bag, which she set down on the floor. Then she removed her carry-bag and her clothes and put them also into the plastic bag. She told Eeelk, "These bags are coated inside with antibiotics and insecticides. We need to keep our interior environment — we call it the 'Inside' — as free of pollution as possible." She zipped the bag closed and put it into a chute door in the wall. A buzzer sounded. Ruth yelled, "Hold your breath!" and they both were sprayed with an insecticide and a full-spectrum antibiotic while being bathed in ultraviolet light by the airlock's decontamination systems.

Not breathing as Humans do, Eeelk experienced the chemical spray as interesting and delicious, and hir many green quasi-chloroplasts reveled in the ultraviolet light, gobbling trillions of high-energy photons.

*   *   *

A few days later at the next open meeting of the Community's Defense Syndic, with Ruth sitting beside hir, Eeelk listened with interest as the Humans governed themselves.

The meeting began with everyone talking at once. The balding middle-aged man serving as Center of the meeting waved his hands in the air and called out, "People! People! Quiet, please! Let me review for our new green friend what we have already done to defend our Community! The rest of you can add whatever I forget."

After calls of "You tell'm, Dave!" from most of the syndic members, David, who was a nephew of Ruth's, addressed himself to Eeelk, speaking loudly enough so everyone in the meeting room could hear:

"Do you know we have a 'no-*man's*-land' of truly ruined, abandoned buildings between our various sealed Communities?"

"Yes," Eeelk answered.

"So, we've been planning – that is *we*, the Defense Syndic of *this* Community — we've been planning what to do if the Boogee-Guards ever came looking for any Guards that members of our Hunters' Syndic unfortunately had to kill —"

"They shouldn't have killed the bot!" a woman yelled-out from the Assembly of the Observers. "Bots are all the Boogees care about!"

"What's done is done, Joyce," David said. "And you need to bring that up at the General Community Meeting next week. Let me finish, all right?"

With irritated grumbling and hoots of anger, the Assembly quieted down. David was a frequent facilitator for the Defense Syndic's meetings, and he held the Syndic-granted rank of '*Colonel*', so he usually had the group well in hand. "What we decided to do," he continued quietly, "was take advantage of the fact that the Boogees will never believe so many of us could have survived Outside the Domes. They have always seen us, the descendants of those who weren't invited into the Domes, as inferior sub-human creatures. And because they are always in competition with each other, they can't understand the reality of our ability to cooperate with one another, our Equality, nor our Solidarity. They believe if there *are* any people of the former Working class still living after centuries, Outside the Domes, they would have to be sick, insane, dying, alone, and mostly male. They believe women are weak and cowardly, you see. Of course, they are wrong about all that. 'Specially bout the women."

Spontaneously, the women in the Assembly, including Ruth, stood up and cheered and whistled for David. Several of the men joined them. Eeelk contemplated the complex dynamics of a species with two genders.

David continued, now in a soft tone of voice so the Assembly had to be quiet to hear him, "Years ago, we built a fake dwelling, a decoy in the half-basement of a derelict house, furnished with rifles and ammunition, rusty cans of food, rat and rabbit bones, and the un-cleaned domestic filth to be expected of an insane old man living alone. We built a supposedly 'accidental thoroughfare' to this man's '*lair*' in the ruins, with dead trees, collapsed buildings, solid piles of rubbish, and abandoned old machines lining the sides.

"Now, since we get both snow and rain in springtime in this area of the world, the next time it rains hard, so there's less chance of any Boogee-Guards being about, we'll drag the dead bodies of those guards Ruth killed to the fake 'thoroughfare' and position them as though an old man had shot them from the 'safety' of his lair —"

"I can help with that!" Eeelk trumpeted excitedly.

"Say what?" David asked.

"Don't you see? It will show on their bodies if you drag them any distance, even in the rain. I can take them inside my body and slither – leaving an almost invisible track of no known earth-animal — to the 'thoroughfare' you have prepared, and arrange the bodies any way you like."

"What you folks think?" David asked the assembly.

The Syndic Members and the Observers roared their approval.

"Okay, Eeelk, sounds good. You *know* we don't need those bodies partially digested —"

"Of course not," Eeelk replied, sounding hurt. "I would never eat a Sapient Being, even one already dead and chewed by rats."

"Of course the sapience of anyone who would work for the Boogees is greatly in doubt," Ruth commented loudly. The Assembly laughed and David gently admonished Ruth, calling her "my favorite, cynical, old Anarkhist-aunt."

David faced the meeting of the Defense Syndic and raised his arms, saying, "Are there any objections to Eeelk helping out as zee indicated zee could?"

There was a long moment of silence as everyone waited for possible objections, since *'Dissent Must Always Be Heard'* was one of their cultural axioms, and then the Assembly enthusiastically clapped for Eeelk.

"All right!" David shouted over the clapping as it began

to die down, "Seven ay-em the next time we have a hard rain! Assemble Inside at the Hunters' Gate!"

*   *   *

In most seasons, despite three hundred years of worldwide climate changes, with the weather disturbed locally by the five-mile-high geodesic-domes of the Boogees, that area of Greater Cleveland, because of its nearness to Lake Erie, was still heavy with precipitation. Two days later, a hard rain had been falling since midnight when warmer winds aloft had melted the snow as it fell.

Ruth assembled with Eeelk and the Defense Syndic at the Hunters' Gate that rainy morning. Colonel David tried to insist his aunt was too old to go out and work in the cold rain.

"I'm wearing a sweater and a rain-parka, David, as you can see," she said, "and I'm just going to be a lookout. I don't plan to do any heavy work." She held up her crossbow. Everyone knew what a great shot she was, and what a keen eye she had for a person of sixty-six.

"All right," David said.

They spent the morning dragging the three corpses off piles of trash on the sidewalks, and redressing them in their clothing and armor. Ragged holes had to be cut out of the clothes over the quarrel holes on the bodies. The fatal wounds were altered to look like bullet holes through and through, leaving no bullet to be found in the body. The armor had to be left unsealed as if the men had been careless, enabling the rats to get to them after they were killed.

Then, one at a time, Eeelk engulfed the corpses into hir body and slithered to the thoroughfare' leading to the false dwelling. Zee dropped each of them to sprawl awkwardly in positions which sold the lie that they had been shot from the relative 'safety' of the false lair.

From her position as lookout, Ruth saw a small group of people come out of the 'Hunters' Gate' carrying a stretcher with a man-sized lump under a waterproof tarp in the rain. They carried the stretcher down the 'thoroughfare' to the half-story-deep basement where the fake lair had been set up.

Later, talking with Eeelk and David in the Geejjikk's 'Nest' — the private cubic the Community had assigned to Eeelk — Ruth asked who had been on the stretcher taken to the false lair.

"Wilken Raysman," David said. "He had this cubic before you, Eeelk. Nice guy. I knew him in the Defense Syndic before he got cancer."

"I thought he was dead," Ruth said.

"No, he's been dying of cancer in our hospital for quite a while now. A solid tumor in his pancreas, very painful. Apparently, they can't operate and remove it. Most the time, he's been nearly comatose with pain meds, but when he heard about Ruth's defense of the Community, he volunteered to be a decoy the Boogee-guards could kill, to satisfy their blood lust. You know, neither the Boogees nor their Guards can even *imagine* the size and viability of our Communities. They think in terms of lone males standing up to a hostile environment. They don't really believe in Cooperation —"

A old, battered, pink, 'princess' phone beside Eeelk's resting-place began to ring. The phone lines were internal and didn't involve radio, which could easily have been overheard by the Boogees. David picked up the phone and listened. "They have something on camera now," he told Ruth and Eeelk. "It's an assault-tank. They're taking the 'thoroughfare!' Wilken is shooting at them! They stopped at the first body, and they've fired their big gun! It's collapsed the house above him. They probably killed him. . . ."

"He must have been in great pain without his meds." Ruth said quietly.

"Yes," David said. "He had to be off his pain-meds in order to operate a rifle —"

"He's shooting at them again!" David interrupted himself. "One of the Guards got out of the tank, and was trying to lift the first body up, and Wilken got him! Oh, now, the Guards are running the tank right toward Wilken's lair. That's it then," David said to Ruth and Eeelk.

"Process the film of that for the next meeting, okay?" David said into the phone. "Thanks."

"The man had courage," Ruth said. "We owe a great debt to his memory."

"Enduring the pain was the hardest part of it, I am sure," David said. "You know what he said to me when they brought him out the Hunters' Gate?"

"What?" Ruth asked.

"He lifted the tarp a little that was keeping him dry, and motioned me over. I bent down to see what he wanted. His voice was raspy and strained. I could hardly hear him over the sound of the rain. He said to me, 'We should have appointed you 'Commodore', not 'Colonel,' hey, Davey?'"

"I told him, 'Sailor, we all appreciate what you're doing.' He replied, 'Better than taking so long to die', and then he turned his head away and dropped the corner of the tarp. I'll never forget the pain in his face."

"We'll have a memorial service, if the Guards are satisfied and leave us alone. And we'll tell the children, for all of our generations, about his courage, and how he saved us," Ruth said.

The radio-listeners from the Defense Syndic soon reported to the Community that the Boogees and their guards were apparently satisfied with the lie of *the lone man hidden in a basement killing three Guards*. Another crisis, one of many, had been averted.

* * *

Eeelk discovered the Community zee had joined had remarkably well-equipped laboratories where zee might do hir own research into the problems concerning hir species. One day, in a laboratory near the private cubic zee had been given, Eeelk met the Coordinator for one of the Communities' laboratories.

LABORATORY "B"
!!! WARNING !!!
POSSIBLE CONTAMINATES
OR LIVE INSECTS
NO ENTRY WITHOUT PROTECTIVE CLOTHING !!!
<<< RING BELL FOR INFO; PLEASE WAIT!

After Eeelk rang the bell, a large male Human with ebony skin-colour wearing an airmask and a long white labcoat stepped out into the hall and said, in a deep voice, "What can I do for you?"

"I am hoping I could use your laboratory facilities for some research of my own," Eeelk said.

"Hmmm, maybe we can help you. How much table space will you need? Have you got any equipment of your own? May I ask what your research is for?"

"I'm not sure how much table space I will need; I have no equipment, only myself; I need to research Geejjikk biochemistry and reproductive processes, because there might not be another Geejjikk on this planet for me to mate with when I am an adult, before I die."

"That's a problem," the big man said.

"Yes. A serious problem, as far as I'm concerned."

"Certainly. Well, come on in. What kind of protective clothing can you wear?"

"I won't need any. Pollutants and the insects will not bother me."

"Something to envy. You're a lucky man . . . uh . . . person. Uh, let me get the door for you."

Eeelk squeaked softly as zee slithered after the large ebony man through a small airlock into the laboratory. The Human put his hand out to touch the Geejjikk, noting hir skin felt somewhat like a rubber balloon.

"How about this table?" The ebony man said, gesturing to an empty table in a corner. "You wouldn't be disturbed here."

"Fine. What equipment may I use?"

"Anything that isn't currently in use or about to be. Just ask. And all the glassware must be washed and sterilized immediately after use. Please don't break anything. What we have is very old and we can't remake anything with the precise volume markings they could in Pre-Dome Times."

"I'll try to use as little glassware as possible. I can do much of the analysis inside my own body."

"Ah, then perhaps we can use you for some of our work certifying meat as safe and edible."

"Yes. I'd be glad to help. I want to be a useful member of the Community."

"Wonderful! Welcome. Umm, my name is Tamir Jefferson. I'm the general coordinator here," the ebony-skinned Human said.

"Eeelk, child of Speet-&-Eeesk." The Geejjikk extruded a pseudopod and formed a green-coloured approximation of a primate hand on the end of it.

Tamir grinned, and shook Eeelk's 'hand'. . . .

*　　*　　*

One day early in their relationship Eeelk and Ruth were lounging together in a common-area near an airlock. Fluorescent lights overhead shone down on neat boxes of decorative, broad-leafed plants with colorful flowers along all the walls. The air was wonderfully heavy with their perfume. The plants helped to maintain a livable level of oxygen Inside where the people lived, and lessened the work of the CO_2 - scrubbers which were spread throughout the sealed dwellings.

"Ruth, why do you-all hunt with a crossbow rather than a rifle?" Eeelk asked.

"You know we're in hiding because we fear the Boogees in the Domes?" She was knitting a cotton baby-blanket of recycled yarn as part of her labor-contribution to the community for that day.

"Yes."

"Rifles are too noisy, and would give away the secret of our existence. Plus, crossbow bolts are much easier for us to manufacture than gunpowder and bullets."

"Ah, I perceive. And crossbows are easier to learn to operate accurately, rather than a longbow and arrows, is that not so?"

"Yes. That's it. I don't have the strength to pull a longbow, but I can pull the trigger on one of our weapons. The hair-trigger Leonardo DaVinci designed so long ago for our crossbows makes it easy for an old woman like me to be a good shot."

"Tell me, my friend," Eeelk asked Ruth. "Why didn't you accept the invitation of my species to go aboard our starships, escape this dying planet, and join the Galactic Community?"

"My husband and all the children we had together are dead."

"That would not have negated our invitation."

"I know, but . . . how can I explain?. . ."

"Perhaps you can begin by explaining to me how your species reproduces. Would you?"

Ruth gave hir a short description of eggs, sperm, women, men, sex, babies, and raising children.

"Did you have all your children at once?" Eeelk asked.

"No. I had five babies, one at a time, in eleven years. Three lived, one was born dead. And ... uh ... the fifth, my youngest, was born maimed, without any epidermis at all – You know? The epidermis is our outer layer of skin – Also he had no anus, two blind eyeballs in one opening in the middle of his forehead, and two deformed penises . . . He cried constantly, obviously in terrible pain. He couldn't nurse. There was nothing anyone could do. We didn't have the medical materials or the skills we needed. He could not live without an epidermis, because — besides the constant pain — he had no protection against infection. The medicos covered him all over with warm rendered chicken fat as soon as he was born, to ease his pain, and so I . . . I could hold him in my arms, showing him how much he was loved. . . . Khkkk," (she cleared her throat), shaking tears from her eyes.

"When he was less than three hours old, after frantic conferences with every medico in our community and those of our immediate neighbors, they gave him a large dose of an opiate which we hoped would give him some feelings of pleasure before a second shot stopped his breathing and, uh . . . killed him." She put her knitting down and wiped the tears from her eyes. "I held him, the poor helpless little thing, and told him I loved him, the whole time."

I am so sorry, Ruth," Eeelk said, extruding a thick pseudopod to embrace the human around her shoulders.

"It's the radioactive dust," she said, "left over from that last war last century, and the pollution . . . My husband and I were lucky three of our children were mostly all right.

But we lost them all, too, later on. When my daughter was sixteen, she was captured by the Boogees. She had such pale skin, you see. She was out hunting. Her companions saw her taken by the Guards into one of those Boogee assault-tanks. We never could find out exactly what had happened to her. Her young husband lost his own life trying to break into those Boogee Domes out in Lake County, where they had probably taken her. Hunters from one of the Communities near the Domes found his bullet-riddled body and brought it back to us. Oh, and both my sons died young of lung cancer. They each had stayed out too long, hunting, many times, after their oxy tanks had run out, and they had breathed in the raw, polluted, unfiltered air of our ruined planet. They thought they were being courageous, so macho, ignoring the danger of that foul air in order to get their job done. Since then, we've had to be much stricter when teaching the children about the dangers of our dystopian environment, and the fatal futility of being carelessly '*brave*'."

"I still don't understand," Eeelk said, "why you refused the chance we offered you to leave Earth and live in a pollution-free environment in the last years of your life."

"I have no descendants. It was better for the room on the ships, and the resources, to go to people who had family to plant on those new worlds you Geejjikk had told us about. And I have nothing familiar now except this Community and the planet of my birth. Dear old Earth."

"I know you were told — I have memories of one of my parents doing so — that there was plenty of room for you, and that the Galactic Civilization also has methods available to all which could extend your life long past the usual limit for your species."

Ruth smiled at Eeelk. "So, that was one of your parents. (He?)(She?) . . . Uh, seemed like such a pleasant, compassionate, uh, person. . . ."

"We Geejjikk are all one gender, you remember. Our language doesn't even have a word for *'gender.'*"

"That's what is most strange about you to us Earthlings, more than you looking like giant green amoebas," Ruth said. She picked up her knitting and continued work.

Eeelk said, "We think any more than one gender is strange. The Djuiivv have three genders, for instance —"

"Tell me about how you Geejjikk reproduce, about your children," Ruth said.

"I have no children, and perhaps never will."

"Oh, that's right. You told me you're very young. Why do you think you won't ever have children?"

"Because there's not another of my species on your Earth, for me to mate with," Eeelk said.

"You mate to have children, even though your species has only one gender? How's that? We'd think you would divide like an earth-amoeba, and reproduce by fission."

"We do, in a sense. We first combine two bodies, in fusion, and then fission into four children. DNA recombination in each generation – like you Humans do – is necessary for a species to produce variety and evolve, is it not?"

"Yes, as I understand it." Ruth sighed heavily, "I wish there was something we could do to help you."

"You are. The Community is. I have been given a space for research in one of your laboratories."

"Do you have the technical skills necessary for research?"

"Yes, inherited from my parents. Speet was a genetic scientist and Eeesk was a bio-technologist."

"You inherit your parents' knowledge *and* manual skills?"

"Yes."

"Sounds like your childhoods must be a bit different from Human-childhoods."

"Yes. I suppose you're right. Since Humans don't inherit their parents' memories, you must spend your childhoods acquiring the knowledge and skills necessary for you to function in your society. Whereas we Geejjikk spend our childhoods talking with our siblings to thereby strengthen and enrich in each of us the memories of all our ancestors. Preserving our racial memory is most important to my species. I can remember happenings back ten million of our years, since before we Geejjikk became sapient."

"Eeelk, I'm impressed. If you ever need the help of a lab-rat, I —"

"No. The labs have plenty of rats. Your hunters are very skilled. The meat must be always flushed of foul air and water, and checked for disease before it can be released to the kitchens. I have abilities I contribute to the Community to make sure the food is safe —"

Ruth laughed. "No, Eeelk, I meant I have some skills as a laboratory *technologist,* and if you ever need help with your research, I'd be glad to contribute my labor."

"Ah. I understand. You're a lab- . . . uh . . . *rat*. Is that the vernacular?"

"Yes. I know English can be a crazy language. . . ."

"All of your Earth-languages are strange in their own ways."

"I suppose so."

A bell chimed quietly, telling them a hunting party was coming Inside through the 'Hunters' Gate'. Eeelk got up and slithered off to help decontaminate the afternoon's catch.

The young hunters, two women and one man, exited the lock, naked, after their decontamination. They greeted Ruth as they hurried past to take a shower with filtered, sterilized, recycled water and get comfortably dressed in their Inside-clothes. Younger people greeted most oldsters with the respectful "Granther," but Ruth had begged to be excluded, because each such greeting just painfully reminded her that she had no grandchildren, and never would. Her sons had lived long enough to have fathered children, but both, apparently, had been sterile. Their widows had tried again with other men and had conceived.

When Eeelk returned from hir snack, the friends resumed their conversation.

"So you have all your parents' memories?" Ruth asked, pulling more yarn from the basket beside her.

"Yes, but some are very dim because I lost the chance to spend my childhood reinforcing all my parental memories by talking about them with my siblings."

"So you are, and are not, a duplicate of your parents?"

"I are not."

"Am not," Ruth corrected hir.

"My English is not perfect?"

"No, but very good for someone relying on dim parental memories."

Could you conjugate the verb for me?"

"I *am;* you *are;* zee, she, he, it *is.* Those are the singular, present-tense forms of the verb, 'to be.'"

"Yes. Thank you. I remember now."

"How many of our Earthly languages can you speak?"

"Several. I'm not sure exactly what they are. They will come to me, I think, nearly intact, whenever I need them. Like English, which I did not think about until I saw you and spoke to you in the language I thought was dominant in this area of your world."

"All from the memories of your parents?"

"Yes. All the members of our expedition learned as many earth languages as possible, so we could communicate effectively with all the Humans on your planet."

"So you saved people from all over the world? Different cultures, races, religions, histories, and colours?"

"The only culture we set out to save was your peaceful world-wide culture of Solidarity and economic-cooperation outside the Domes of the obviously competitive and violent Capitalists. We didn't care about religions or minor customs, although I believe various small groups of Humans were determined to save their religions, their unique ethnic customs, and languages. And as far as colour goes, you are all, to us, one colour: various shades of brown melanin. We Geejjikk are various shades of green quasi-chlorophyll. Variety is interesting, is it not?"

"Yes, Eeelk. And you yourself bring us a very interesting

variety of colour and form. I'm glad you came to us, rather than living alone and lonely outside our Community."

"Lonely? Yes, I was. Not any more, however."

"Good. I'm glad you like Humans."

"So am I."

*   *   *

The years of Earth went by. The Community dug more tunnels to other buildings still standing in their area, and Humans of both genders, working in air masks, converted those buildings to sealed dwellings (at slight over-pressure, to keep out the foul air of dying-Earth) to make workshops, bedrooms, classrooms, and food factories.

A well-equipped expedition of young people, accompanied by Eeelk, was sent to Lake Erie, the nearest Great Lake, to see if surviving fish or anything useful could be had from those waters long ago polluted with sewage, radioactive waste, and chemical sludge. Using Eeelk's ability to "taste" the genetic and chemical components of living organisms, the expedition had to conclude that probably all the Great Lakes were too polluted to provide a viable ecosystem for plants or animals compatible with Human digestion. All the food the Community needed would have to come from mutated free-range rats or rabbits and those vegetable-organisms long ago rescued from the collapsing biosphere.

Carefully avoiding being seen by well-armed roving gangs of Guards — who prowled the 'slums' for reasons known only to their Boogee-employers — running-messengers were dispatched, carrying extra oxy-nitrogen tanks, to share information with the Sovereign Communities whose territory touched theirs all around. The sad news of the irrecoverable death of the American Great Lakes would spread out around the world like ripples in a pond. They had received the terrible news of the death of the Black and the Caspian Seas in exactly the same way. Eeelk added news of hir abandonment, and asked if any other Geejjikk were still on Earth.

The Communities between the Boogee-Domes, worldwide, never used radio or microwaves to communicate. Nothing of the size and the viability of the Co-operative Communities of Human beings Outside the Domes could be revealed to the violent and greedy inhabitants living inside the Domes, lest they try to re-colonize the 'slums' between the Domes, and re-enslave the people.

Former members of the Working class had been meant to starve and disappear when the Boogees had built robots to replace them. The struggles more than two centuries before, when all their jobs had disappeared, worldwide — and the violent reprisals against the hungry and homeless unemployed by those in the Domes who owned the factories and the robots – had taught all the people living Outside the Domes that the Boogees — although Human like themselves — were their mortal enemies. Living in peace with the ultra-privileged Dome dwellers, except as slaves whose lives were worth nothing, was clearly impossible.

*   *   *

Ruth, like many Community members, had adopted a workstyle with a revolving schedule of different jobs essential to the smooth running of the Community. They were mostly unpleasant or tedious tasks no one wanted to do for very long. Ruth and Eeelk remained friends, and they often worked together, when zee was not busy in hir research laboratory, at tasks where they could talk, sing, or laugh together.

One week they worked on sewage reclamation, enjoying the extra use of soap and the long hot showers shit-Workers were entitled to. To Eeelk, soap was a tasty, sensuous experience on hir differently permeable skin, and zee giggled whenever zee showered.

The next week they pedaled bicycles every evening shift in the basement of a large building, providing electricity to much of the Community in that immediate area. The Human bicyclists were always delighted to see Eeelk, a big green blob, balanced on a thin bicycle seat while two thick, green, well-muscled extrusions worked the pedals. Eeelk entertained hir bicycling companions by trumpeting — often with full 'orchestra accompaniment' — all the music zee had learned from carefully hoarded disks stored in the Community Library. One of Eeelk's grandparents had been a skilled and popular musician in Geejjikk galactic-society.

Ruth and Eeelk did their share of work together in the Quarantine Laboratory, working with waldos in sealed rooms to sterilize clothing, weapons, and empty oxy-bottles brought in from the Outside.

Eeelk, who never slept, remained always available to remove fleas from dead rats or rabbits. Or to eat pieces of meat in the Pre-kitchen Laboratories to identify those animals which were free of disease and could be used immediately for food. Eeelk enabled the pre-kitchen laboratories to give up much of their tedious viral, chemical, and antibody testing to screen food from the Outside before releasing it to be eaten by the Community. Eeelk particularly had first taste of any rabbits brought in by the hunters. Rabbits were subject to plague from fleas, like the Humans and the rats, and also to Tularemia, a disease fatal to Humans which had been released into the wild rabbit population more than two centuries before in an effort by the Boogees to kill off the last of their former employees whom they no longer had any use for.

Eeelk and hir friend occasionally worked on one of the basement farms during the busy harvest times. Ruth did not much like the work, which was mostly stoop labor, except for picking fruit from dwarf fruit trees, which she could do standing up. Eeelk was best at picking fruit because zee could employ more than two 'arms' at once. Multiple arms meant zee was also best at folding laundry when they worked in one of the Community's communal laundries. . . .

Both Ruth and Eeelk often enjoyed the quiet work of tending the community fish farm, housed in shallow water-trenches covering the floor of a large one-story building which had been one of the first "food factories" the Community had sealed off from the polluted Outside environment. Subsequent genetic experimentation by their scientists had produced several varieties of fish to enhance the food supply.

The factory was quiet, dimly lit and humid. The fish

were silent, swimming unconcerned in their trenches. Humans walked amid the trenches, long lightweight poles tipped with small fish nets in their hands. They transferred newly born fish into their own trenches, away from the larger fish who might eat them. They also occasionally captured caviar when the experts in charge of the fish farm decided it was appropriate.

The rhythm of Community work filled the days between those times Ruth could go Outside to hunt rats and rabbits.

Eeelk worked with increasing feelings of helplessness at hir laboratory bench. Zee discovered again and again that hir reproductive potential needed to be stimulated from outside hir own body. All of Eeelk's research pointed to the frustrating truth that zee could not reproduce alone.

After work, Eeelk and Ruth enjoyed the times of large-scale Community celebrations which nearly everyone attended. The Community enjoyed basketball, soccer and field hockey games played in a large gymnasium building which was part of their Community Space. There were tournaments with other neighboring communities, and other celebrations to enliven their lives Inside, away from the dangers of their ruined biosphere. Both Eeelk and Ruth watched, with a deep sense of personal loss, the young people at their games.

Once, during the time she and Eeelk were becoming close friends, Ruth was asked to move from her cubic. A large extended family had been found living in isolation not too far from the Community, and had been invited to join. The new family had wanted to live all together, as they always had. Moving Ruth and a few others who were willing was the easiest solution.

Ruth did not mind moving. She thought of all the Community's space as *home.* She had moved within it several times in her life, and it had always cheered her with thoughts of new possibilities and new neighbors.

A tall, smiling, young, light-brown-skinned woman from the extended family had offered to help Ruth transfer her things to her new cubic, pulling a hand-truck with some of the old woman's meager possessions on it, mostly her personally-owned books. And Eeelk accompanied them, to provide Ruth with a familiar 'face' while she was changing her immediate environment.

On a busy workday, the Humans walked and Eeelk slithered the main 'thoroughfare' of the Community, across the concrete floors of old basements and through packed-dirt-paved tunnels connecting the old buildings. Often, the basements served as dirt farms growing — besides dwarf fruit trees — vegetables, berries, spices, or medicinal herbs under fluorescent lights, and the concrete path they walked was two feet below the soil of the farms. Occasionally, a deeper basement was a metals workshop. Humans riding stationary bicycles supplied the lathes, drills, and table-saws with electricity. The sound of their industry was muffled and hidden from any possible Boogee-Guards roving nearby by the depth and thickness of the earth all around, by insulated ceilings, and by the sturdy, insulated doors blocking sound from echoing down the tunnels.

Every Worker they passed greeted Eeelk and Ruth pleasantly. Both of them were well-known and well-liked as individuals in the Community. The new woman from the extended family which had recently joined the Community was welcomed and told about work needs and social opportunities by several of the young farmers in the basements they passed through.

After what turned out to be a short, cheery stroll-and-slither, they reached the building where Ruth had been invited to live. It was a sealed, old, 'inner-city' Victorian house which appeared from the Outside to be a total burned-out wreck. Any snooping 'guards' who rumbled by in their military tanks or on foot — oblivious to the hidden industry all around them in the well-insulated, apparently ruined neighborhood — could only see the total devastation they expected. Actually, the Victorian's deep basement was crammed with bicycles in heavy use supplying electricity for much of that section of the Community. People pedaled furiously together and talked or sang in the heavily-insulated space with others pedaling closely around them.

Ruth and her companions went upstairs to the first floor of the house, passing through the kitchen where several Humans were preparing supper for their housemates as well as the electrical Workers laboring below them on the bicycles.

A dark-skinned woman Ruth's apparent age introduced herself as "Teresa Alvarez," and showed them Ruth's new cubic on the first floor of the old house: "There are shelves beside the fireplace for your books," she told Ruth. "We hope it's all right to continue to store the house books there in your room. It used to be our library. . . ."

"Oh, no," Ruth said. "I don't want to take any communal space you're using —"

"We don't use it much, except to go in and out to get a book, so you can have it for your cubic. If you don't mind someone coming in now and then?"

"No, of course not. All those books make great decor. Do you have any kids in the house?"

"We have three, two of them my . . . uh . . . grandkids. I'm sorry. We . . . um . . . know how it is with you. . . ."

"That'll be great. I love to have kids around. People I can introduce to new ideas and stories, now I seem to have finished Eeelk's education. Just have everybody call me Ruth, instead of 'Granther,' okay?"

"Yes, certainly. Will Eeelk be visiting you often?"

"I hope so," Eeelk answered for hirself, sliding hir bulk upwards to hir full nine feet of extension and still not touching the old fashioned ceiling. "Will that be all right, Teresa?"

"Yes. The kids will brag to their friends about how often they get to see you, Eeelk. Really, our whole household is looking forward to having Ruth here with us, and your visits will always be a special treat. Can you stay for supper?"

"Yes, I can. Thanks," Eeelk said.

Ruth smiled at Teresa. "You have already made me feel so very welcome here. Thank you." She looked around her new cubic, her new bedroom.

"Okay!" Teresa walked over to the door into the next room. "Long ago, someone blocked off this old Victorian arch with its sliding pocket-doors and put in a sound-proofed wall and a door, which you can keep closed when you want some privacy."

"I see the dining room is right outside my cubic. Very convenient," Ruth said.

"And now it's time to eat," Theresa said. Several people had arrived in the dining room for supper.

The house schedule that evening was a combined workday evening meal and a celebration of Ruth's arrival. The three children living in the house sang a song about a sad little dragon who had trouble cooking dinner with his fiery breath, which they had learned in school when Ruth had been their substitute music teacher, and she was delighted to hear it sung so well. Eeelk protested zee had never been taught that particular song. Ruth, Teresa, and the kids promised to teach hir when next zee came to visit them.

Dinner was a cold soup with crunchy vegetables on the side, and toasted home-baked bread made from the Community's grain grown several basements away. The bicyclists ate in two shifts until an evening crew came to relieve them all.

After dinner, Ruth retired to her new bedroom, to settle-in. Eeelk had earlier been summoned back to the Hunters' Gate by telephone.

* * *

Several weeks later, one Friday, Eeelk spent the day working, without Ruth as hir partner, in the Pre-kitchen Laboratories, 'tasting' rabbits and rats to screen them for disease. In the evening, zee stopped by Ruth's domicile to have supper with Ruth and her housemates. Eeelk had a standing invitation.

A large man with tightly curled black hair and dark skin was in the kitchen cooking when Eeelk slithered up from the basement. "Oh, Eeelk," he said, turning slightly from a bowl of something he was vigorously whisking. It was Tamir Jefferson, coordinator of the laboratory where Eeelk had space to do hir research. "Ruth will not be here this evening," he said. "She's gone to have a Sabbath meal with her Jewish friendship group, and then they'll go on to Synagogue together. She'll be back late."

"How could I *not* have known, all these years, that Ruth is religious?" Eeelk asked.

"She isn't much, I think. Once in a while she likes to go to Jewish services, to say some special prayer for her deceased husband, I guess. She was raised Classic Reformed . . . no, *Reform* . . . by her parents, as I understand it. Starting with our Grandparents and Great-Grandparents, most of us Humans have tried to cling to some religious or ethnic identity, ever since we had to begin this new way of life, living Inside, conserving rare resources, hiding from the Boogees, and cooperating with other Humans whom our ancestors had once looked-upon as strangers."

"You Humans are so complex. Could I stay for supper anyway?"

"Certainly. The kids'll be delighted. As will we all."

*   *   *

One spring day, just before Ruth's eighty-first birthday, she was Outside with a hunting party of young people, who were hoping to pick up a few tricks from the master. Eeelk slithered close beside Ruth. Everyone knew they were special friends.

"I hope we encounter no Guards today. I know that each time we have to kill Guards to protect ourselves, we increase the chances of our being discovered," Eeelk said quietly.

"Those damned Boogees haven't the faintest idea our existence is possible," Ruth snarled, also quietly.

"Never underestimate the enemy, my friend."

"I know. I know. You're right, of course. But how can you be so wise about all this — about us and the Boogees — if your galactic civilization has no enemies, as you've told me?"

"I have racial memories which go back to my species' distant past, when we were savage and barely-civilized, fighting with each other and our environment for material and territorial advantages. I can remember having enemies, and constant worldwide warfare in order to survive. All the sapient species of the galaxy learned before they left their home planets that freedom and cooperation are the only way to be truly civilized, and the most enduring."

"That racial-memory stuff is better than our history books, isn't it?"

"I suppose so. But my memories are not as keen as what I've read of your history in books. You have detailed information on the Human past gleaned from historical correspondence, contemporary writings, and archeology."

"Perhaps a combination of techniques would work best," Ruth said.

"I will not be able to pass on my memories unless I am able to Reproduce, and the information we have gotten back from message-runners is that there is not another Geejjikk on Earth to mate with me, so I will probably never Reproduce," Eeelk said sadly. "Solitary living is not the way of my species."

"Won't your people ever come back looking for you?" Ruth's attention was suddenly fixed on a rat skulking through the ruins nearby.

"No. The Barrier to keep the competitive, aggressive, potentially genocidal Boogee-Humans out of the rest of the galaxy has already been set in place around your star-system, between the distant globular Oort Cloud and the closer-in Kuiper Belt."

"Oh. You never mentioned that," Ruth mumbled, double-checking that her crossbow was armed.

"I didn't think of it until just now."

"Parental memories?"

"Yes."

"So you and I will just have to grow very old together, both of us without offspring," Ruth said quietly, watching the rat.

"I will not grow old," Eeelk whispered. "I will dissolve."

"What?" Forgetting the rat, Ruth quickly shifted her attention to concentrate on her globular green friend.

"I will dissolve."

"We will lose you?"

"Yes."

"We can't let that happen."

"It can't be stopped. It is the natural way of my species. Didn't you know that much of my research was aimed at increasing my lifespan so I could survive with my memories intact until I could find a mate?"

"Hasn't your remarkable species as yet figured out a way for you to live longer and breed on a slower schedule?"

"As civilized Geejjikk, for hundreds of your millennia now, we have been able to modify our biochemical processes so that we live much longer as adults, and do not double our population so very quickly. But I was never given the modifications, since I was too young when I lost touch with my people."

"Maybe our biochemists can figure out something —"

"No," Eeelk trumpeted sadly. "The process is very advanced and complicated. I concluded with my research that Human biochemistry cannot change the way my species is built, and I do not myself have the knowledge of Geejjikk biochemistry needed to extend my lifetime. Besides, it would have had to be done when I was much younger."

"How does Reproduction work for your people, without biochemical modification?"

"We are born as *Four* new individuals from the Reproductive Act of our parents. Without modification so we live much longer as adults, we live as individuals for about twenty of our years, consolidating our parents' memories and then finding our own. When we are fully mature, we conjugate with another of our species to whom we have become emotionally attached, and we share and intertwine our genetic material. We split after our Reproductive Fusion with another and become *Four* who . . . and so forth. The process is nearly impossible to interrupt or modify."

"Eeelk, do you mean that you disappear when you produce children?"

"Yes, but *I* will not. If I cannot form a Reproductive Fusion with another of my kind, and share my genetic material, I will dissolve into a chaotic green goo you will have to mop up and flush down a drain to Waste Reclamation. Nothing can prevent that."

"We've been friends for over fifteen earth-years now, haven't we," Ruth asked, suppressing the panic she suddenly felt.

"Yes," Eeelk answered.

"How soon are you going to have to dissolve, one way or the other?"

"Soon. The urge to Reproduce has been with me now for some time. Twenty of our years are only about fifteen of yours."

She made a sudden decision. "Tomorrow we'll see a doctor," Ruth said.

"There is nothing your species' doctors can do for me."

"Tomorrow, a doctor," Ruth said firmly. "You haven't tried that option yet, I'm sure. It is best to know all about a problem before you try to solve it."

"But –"

"Nope, not another word. We'll see a doctor." Ruth thought she might have an answer, but she didn't want to get Eeelk's hopes up. *So pragmatic, the Geejjikk . . .*

she thought. *If zee is typical of hir species. Oh well, we'll see. . . .*

*   *   *

After all the testing had been done on a small piece of Eeelk's green flesh and on a blood sample taken from Ruth, Doctor Davis called Ruth and Eeelk up from their temporary work riding bicycles in the basement of the Community Hospital. The doctor was a handsome young man with kinky auburn hair, dark-hazel eyes, and light brown skin. He took them into his office next to the Genetics Laboratory, had them sit down — *if that position could be said to apply to a Geejjikk*, the doctor thought —and sat himself behind his desk with a few print-outs spread in front of him. "Ruth," he began, "I am happy to tell you that the Geejjikk carry their genetic information as DNA very similar to Humans. Apparently, Eeelk did no research hirself comparing Geejjikk to Human."

"Wonderful!" Ruth said. "I hadn't dared to hope —" (In fifteen years, Eeelk had never considered researching *Human* reproductive mechanisms.)

"What is this all about?" Eeelk asked.

"Well. . . ." the doctor said, looking at Ruth with one eyebrow raised.

"Eeelk," Ruth said, turning to touch her friend's firm, rubbery flesh. Eeelk created a shinny black, convex patch on hir skin facing Ruth which she knew to be an eye of sorts. "Eeelk, Would you, uh, uh. . . ." she stuttered, "w-w-wuh . . . would you . . . uh . . . do the Reproductive Act with me?"

"What?" Eeelk asked, still confused.

"Make babies with me, you dummy!" Ruth exclaimed. "You know I've always had trouble *not* thinking of you as a male, because I'm almost entirely heterosexual, and here you go acting like a typical dumb man. . . ."

"Hey. . . ." Doctor Davis said.

"What?" Eeelk said again. In all fairness, the overwhelming need to Reproduce had been filling hir mind for several days, and zee was understandably distracted.

"I love you, you big green blob! I want to make babies with you!"

"We are not the same species, Ruth, my dear friend."

"Actually," said the doctor, "Ruth was hoping that perhaps the creative process of trying to mix your DNA with Ruth's will enable you to produce at least one offspring, with the same DNA as yourself, having all your personal memories, and save you from sterile dissolving."

"Oh, Ruth," Eeelk said. "My sweet friend. . . ."

"The Community has become accustomed, these last fifteen years," Ruth said, "to you and to all you can do and share with us. We don't want to lose you. *I* don't want to lose you." Ruth had tears in her eyes.

"Ruth, it would kill you," Eeelk said.

"I am an old woman now, with I don't know how many months or years left to live. It would be a meaningful death to me to help you not die in vain, childless. We want you to be able to pass on all the memories you have been gathering for your people."

Eeelk extruded a wide pseudopod and put it around Ruth's shoulders. "Thank you, my dear friend, but I cannot trade your life for mine. I love you too, you . . . you inflexibly-shaped old primate."

"Oh, Eeelk, please reconsider. I might die soon, anyway."

"If I might interrupt," the doctor cut in. "Eeelk, I understand you can perceive plant and animal genomes directly by taking them into your body. Yes?"

"Yes."

"Then why don't we give you some of Ruth's blood? Will you be able to tell if you could safely and creatively combine with her genome rather than another Geejjikk's?"

"All right." Eeelk said. "I don't think it will work, but I will reserve judgment."

Eeelk disappeared into Laboratory 'B' for several days of frenzied research until zee was satisfied that the mixing of hir DNA with Ruth's would actually be successful and make both of them parents, together. Then zee found Ruth and told her the good news.

At the dinner table in Ruth's commune that evening, they told Ruth's housemates about their plan.

"No! Please, Eeelk! Don't do that with Ruth. She'll die!" white-haired Teresa said, near hysterical with shock.

Tamir Jefferson and the other household members also voiced their objections. The children sat and squirmed, open-mouthed, not understanding the sudden flood of adult emotion.

"My friends," Ruth said quietly. "You know I have no descendants. I am an old woman, and this is my last chance to reproduce. It's a way for me to die a meaningful death. And it's the *only* way we can save Eeelk. Please do not begrudge me this opportunity."

"Eeelk, if *you* will not die, how can you do this to your friend?" Tamir asked.

"I will die too, but the combination of our genes and our memories will live on in our children," Eeelk replied.

"I am sorry, my friends," Ruth said. "But death comes to us all. My religion tells me that I have, as a *birth*right, a portion in *the-world-to-come*. By combining my DNA with Eeelk's, I will also have a portion in the future of our Cooperative, multi-coloured civilization, in this life, here on Earth. Please allow me the chance to do this thing for my good friend, Eeelk. Be easy. Don't be sad for me. I'm happy."

"*We* are not happy," Teresa said, "We will *not* be happy." She looked away from Eeelk and Ruth and angrily shook her head. "But. . . . perhaps we can learn to adjust to losing you both. When?"

"We thought to attempt the Reproductive Act tomorrow afternoon in Ruth's cubic," Eeelk said. "I will die very soon if I do not breed."

"You all must promise not to knock on my door for a book tomorrow afternoon and interrupt us," Ruth said. "But for now, I would like to hear the children sing that little dragon song for me, one last time, if they would."

The after-dinner singing and story-telling went on and on and on that evening. When it came time for the younger people to go to sleep, Ruth kissed them tenderly and asked them all to Share happily and grow up to be good,

Co-operative citizens, enjoying their culture's Solidarity. Eeelk, in the shape of a six-legged green pony, gave all the children a ride up to bed. Then the adults stayed up longer, encouraging Ruth to reminisce about her life for them. Eeelk recalled hir meeting with Ruth in humorous detail. The housemates all hid their tears inside their laughter.

*   *   *

"Um, I think I should be on top," Ruth said. "I might become panic-stricken if you're on top and I can't breathe. It probably won't work if I'm not calm and happy. Right?" She was sitting naked on the edge of her bed the next afternoon. Eeelk was spread over it, like an amorphous green blanket.

"Yes. It should feel like good sex to you. Will this extrusion help?" zee asked.

"Oh, yes. Except for the green colour, it looks very realistic. How did you know?"

"I once pretended to be a blanket . . ."

"You shameless voyeur! Who was it?"

"'Who was it?' Now *who* is the voyeur?" Zee rippled with amusement. "It was two young men. They seemed to be well practiced. I felt an obligation to study your species in all its activities, for *my* species' posterity."

"So you could pass that knowledge on to your children?"

"*Our* children, dear friend." Relaxed and content, Eeelk oozed over Ruth's bed. Zee appeared to be a large, amorphous, green 'pancake' except for a small speaking trumpet and one Human-looking extrusion.

"Oh Eeelk! Our children! *Our* children!" Ruth cried.

'Darling Ruth. . ."

"Dear Eeelk."

"Little malleable primate," the Geejjikk trumpeted softly.

"We need lube, lots of lube. . . ." It had been more than three hundred years since artificial sexual lubrication had been manufactured on Earth. Ruth picked up a warm bowl of rendered chicken fat nearby on the floor, applied the lube to Eeelk's '*male*' extrusion, and enfolded it into herself. "Oh, yes. Ah, good. Can you make lips for me to kiss?"

"Sure."

Ruth was eighty-one. She hadn't had sex with a male in nearly thirty years since before her husband had died. She discovered her aged body had forgotten nothing at all about the mechanics and the resolution of heterosexual pleasure.

The yearning to blend herself with her lover which had usually preceded her own orgasm now helped Ruth to eroticize the pain of all her cells coming unstuck from one another and the nuclei of each cell giving up its DNA to the creative soup of Eeelk and the Reproductive Act. She didn't notice when she stopped breathing and Eeelk rolled over on top of her. The Geejjikk spread hirself thin, rolling them both up and making Ruth's permuted body the filling of a giant green '*burrito*.' Ruth's soul cried out with ecstasy as her small, wrinkled body dissolved completely into Eeelk's, and oblivion overcame her.

Barely conscious hirself, giddy with ecstasy, Eeelk unwound and recombined the trillions of DNA strands of both hirself and hir beloved Ruth throughout their combined body, assigning to each potential child an equal portion of the genetic joining with hir Human-mate, and an equal part of what had once been the mitochondria of Ruth's brain cells, where, presumably, the designs were stored for the neural connections of her Human memories.

Finally, bursting with love and hope, Eeelk, too, gave hirself up to oblivion.

*   *   *

The *Four* unwound from each other. They made several black, shiny, convex spots for eyes and looked at the siblings their parents had created. They were each a pale greenish-brown in colour, with a height-extension of only three-and-a-half feet, about a foot shorter than ordinary Geejjikk children. One extruded a trumpet-mouth and spoke in English, which they all knew would henceforth be the primary language among their *Four*. "We have a dinner date with our housemates, don't we?"

"Yes," another said. "This is a good nest, but we can come back to it."

They slithered to the door. One extruded a pseudopod, reached up and turned the knob, and they exited their nest into the dining room. Humans of several body sizes and shades of melanin were gathering for dinner.

"Hello," said one of the Hu-Geejjikk (a new species). "I am Reelk, one of *Four*. Our parents were Eeelk and the brave Human, Ruth Green."

Teresa walked in from the kitchen with a steaming casserole in her hot-mitted hands. Her face was a moving kaleidoscope of grief and curious delight. "Hello, there. We're all glad to see you." She cleared her clogged throat, "Khkkk." For a fleeting moment, her face twisted with anguish. . . .

His deep voice rumbling, Tamir asked quietly, "Then the Reproductive Act went well?"

"Yes. I am Reeth. I happily remember how each of my parents was fond of you all."

"We're hungry, of course. I am Morris. That was Ruth's husband's name."

"Well," Tamir said, taking the casserole from Teresa, "we have a hot vegetable and ming-fish casserole tonight, and rhubarb pie for desert. Also, Teresa invited Rabbi Howard Aaronson here tonight as a guest." The Rabbi was a bright-eyed young man with curly black hair, a short beard, and olive-colored skin.

"Wonderful. We're glad to see him. I am Theer."

"Why am I here?" the Rabbi asked Teresa.

"We thought you might want to say a prayer for Ruth. She . . . *khkkk* . . . died tonight, helping Eeelk create these four little Geejjikk," Teresa said. "Our feelings are very mixed, here in this household. For even though we are glad to see *Four* new Geejjikk —"

"Hu-Geejjikk," Theer said.

All right, Hu-Geejjikk," Teresa said, shaking her head irritably. "We, uh . . . we will miss Eeelk and Ruth, whose fused bodies, as we understand it, fissioned into these *Four* little ones you see here now. They are the new members of our household."

"I will need nine other Jews to say Kaddish for Ruth properly. Perhaps —"

"Only five more are needed," one of the *Four* said. Reeth, probably.

"Eh?" the Rabbi said.

"Are we not Jews, we Four, if our mother, Ruth, was Jewish?" Theer asked.

"Well, uh, I'm not sure," the Rabbi said. "The problem of whether or not sapient non-Humans can be Jewish has never come up before, that I know of. Of course, 'In the Image of God' could logically mean sapience — that is, *intelligence* — not actual physical form. . . .

"You will certainly need to be given a Jewish education," he continued. "I will have to consult the Talmud . . . and my colleagues. . . ." The Rabbi leaned back in his seat, very happily perplexed.

"Let's eat!" Morris cried. "I love ming-fish casserole." Zee extruded a pseudopod and grasped a wineglass stem with a pale greenish-brown version of Ruth's slim-fingered hand. Raising the full glass of red wine, zee sang:

בָּרוּךְ אַתָּה יְיָ אֱלֹהֵינוּ מֶלֶךְ הָעוֹלָם בּוֹרֵא פְּרִי הַגָּפֶן

"Blessed are you, Creator our God,
Master of the Universe —". . .

book two
SPACE TRAVEL

*   *   *

SHIP'S LOG, AUDIO

"Is the recorder on? They put so many buttons at my fingertips; how the hell can I tell which does what? Testing. Testing. Uh. Okay.

"I wish I'd stopped taking that damned consultant-fee from the Family. I had enough money to live carefully in reasonable comfort without it since my first book— _The Twenty-First Century: A Turning Point_, by _Bradley Darsen_—was successful. But I was greedy. I wanted the extra income, and I didn't want to move out of the subsidized Darsen Family Apartments, where I've lived since I left my father's house.

"I have no _real_ talent for business enterprise and will probably never again have a best-selling book. My areas of expertise are too academic to interest the average man. While history and anthropology fascinate me, they give me little chance to make an honest business profit.

"So I kept the usual retainer the Darsen Family gives _all_ its young men when they finish basic schooling, to keep us in moderate comfort until we can make our own unique contribution to the success of the Family business interests. This custom frequently leads to profits for the

Darsen Family as well as to a raise in Family status for the ingenious young entrepreneur. Some guys, who know they have no business skills, take the consultant-fee their whole lives. I had planned to.

"But how was I to know the Darsen Family would find a way through that Barrier the damned Galactics put around our solar system and that *my father would then move immediately to capture the field of interstellar commerce?*

"My father is the Family's Third Vice-President for Interstellar Marketing, a position created over a hundred years ago by my triple-great-grandfather, the family CEO at that time, after my triple-great uncle found in orbit of Saturn a derelict galactic interstellar starship powered by a new kind of drive, the Q-V Drive. A team of Prole-engineers employed by the Family figured out how it worked, and our bots built duplicates.

"Since those unknown galactic aliens put the damned Barrier up, there has been no interstellar marketing for the 3VP to manage. Nevertheless, the 3VP has remained a part of the Family's corporate structure, including all the power that goes with such a position. My father can assign Family consultants (*like me*), transfer Prole-technical-experts, re-assign bots, and purchase other equipment.

"My father was anxious to demonstrate to his relatives— including the current CEO of the Family, his uncle—that his genetic line is good for business. He decided he could use an historical anthropologist—who just happened to be his nearly-worthless over-educated youngest son—to sniff out potential resources in territory out among the stars. As a consultant on retainer, I was obligated to take any job he offered me, however ghastly. Dad almost sent my nephew, Tod, my eldest brother's oldest, but I suppose I was more expendable.

"Aaaaaahh—I'm tired of lying here at three-gees doing nothing — feeling three times heavier than I am on Earth — in this damned waterbed, staring at a sterile, boring, metal ceiling festooned with pipes carrying fluids or electrical wires. *Whatever. . . .*"

"Expendable. Shit. Now I am I don't know *how* many billions of miles from Earth, billions of miles from my cozy suite in the Family Apartments, billions, trillions of miles from my big bookcases crammed with my own personal choice of books, trillions of miles from a brisk fifteen minute walk through the resurrected-Elm trees to the Darsen Family femhouse, where I could have sex and a massage from my pretty teenage-wife any time I wanted. Now, instead, I'm surrounded by total emptiness, by God-damned vacuum! And I'm alone in this ship with no other men for company, not even a Prole-repairman in case something breaks and I haven't got the right kind of bot to fix it.

"They drugged me up when they put me into this thing. I don't even remember leaving Dad's office, or the shuttle trip to wherever they had this new interstellar ship docked before they launched it with my unconscious body strapped into this damned fancy waterbed.

"How long have I been lying here? I'm hungry. My back itches. I need a bath.

"Alpha Centauri. I don't know anything about it. Not my

field of expertise. What the hell do I care about spaceships and stars?

"Let me call one of the bots to put a screen on the ceiling where I can read some stuff about this damned mission Dad sent me on. I hope somebody thought to include a Library for the luckless passenger.

"Is this the right button?"

"So, Alpha Centauri is a triple-star, or maybe only a double-star system. Apparently, the reason Earth's star system doesn't have its own wormhole is because wormholes—a permanent part of the structure of the galaxy—are only found near star systems which have a much greater mass than our own, unusual, *single*-star system. And since most of the mass—*weight,* to us non-scientific types—of a star system is in the star itself, more than one star is usually necessary to generate the gravitic-conditions in local space necessary to have a wormhole. It's all hidden there in Einstein's equations of General Relativity, they say. Lah-dee-dah.

"So I've been ordered to go to Alpha Centauri, which is—let's see—four point three-five lightyears—about twenty-six trillion miles—away from Earth, through the horribly empty vacuum which surrounds me now, to use a wormhole which will take me to another star-system on the other side of that wormhole, somewhere else in the galaxy, many lightyears away. Whatever the hell a lightyear is.

Once there, I have to sniff out the territory, any possibly habitable planets, and their resources, and prepare for reinforcements from the Family. If at all possible, we will take over, with lots of bots, the first planet we find, and use it as a base of operations for the conquest of nearby star-systems where there might be resources the Darsen family can claim, and Galactics—damned squishy aliens—whom we can trade with, sell to, or maybe enslave to increase the Family's profits.

"The bot who brought me the Library screen told me that in an hour, ship's time, the acceleration will drop to one-gee—letting me feel as though I am inside the gravitational field of Earth, at normal weight—for two hours so I will have time to eat, eliminate wastes, and shower. No room nor weight allowance for the '*luxury*' of a bathtub.

"I must have been out a long time, from the drugs, after they launched this damned spaceship. I hope tasty food is not a 'luxury,' even though right now I could eat something like a sawdust sandwich wrapped in old shoe leather. I am ravenous. How many days? or weeks? has it been? When I woke up, I had an old-fashioned IV in my arm, and the food-bag above me on the stand was empty. How long did I lie here unconscious at three-gees—pressed down by three times my normal weight—with my stomach getting emptier and emptier? I could have died of starvation. Or dehydration. Damn my father.

"Uh, apparently, the bot said "ship's time" because the ship is now going fast enough—close to the speed of light—so that time, for us, in the ship, is now flowing much more slowly than it does on Earth. I don't understand Einstein-stuff like that at all. Scientific *gobble-de-goook*. At least it means, as I understand it, that it will *not* take me over four years to reach Alpha Centauri, at least not by how I perceive time inside this spaceship. Great, but none of the bots here are the kind of bots who can tell me *exactly* how long I'm going to be in this damned ship, weighed down in an uncomfortable waterbed by three times my normal weight; let up to eat, shower, and 'eliminate' only two hours out of every twelve.

"Fuck this shit. I am an academic, a student of history and anthropology, not an adventurer, not a businessman trained to look for resources. I am a slave to my father's ambitions.

"Ahummmm. Three gees make me want to sleep all the time. . . ."

"Ugh, the change-of-gee-alarm sounds terrible, but the lessening of weight is wonderful. Now to see if the food on this torture-ship is any good."

"Three gees is a lot worse after two hours at only one-gee. At least the food was good. I hope my stomach is not going to be upset. I'll have to learn to eat faster, so the damned alarm-warning does not catch me with a full stomach.

"Ulllpp. Uh crap. Ughhhhhhhhkhkhkhkhkkkggg . . .

"'Clean-up! Bots! I need clean-up!'

"Ugh. There damned well better be a cleaning-bot. Vomiting at three gees is worse than I could ever have imagined. I nearly drowned.

"Good, here it is. 'Clean it now. Vacuum up the vomit. Don't touch me. Spray me with water. Warm water! And the bed. Yes, that's it. Ah. Yes, take the shirt off and wash it. Bring me another.'"

"Well, if I have to lie here for whatever part of four years I have to be on this ship, I might as well make some substantial notes for my next book. At least, it'll help pass the time.

"The title will be The Twenty-Second Century: Consolidation of Power. The word "power" in the title ought to create some interest, and it is obviously a sequel to my first book, the popular The Twenty-First Century: A Turning Point by Bradley Everett Darsen, a Darsen Press International exclusive. Tah-dah!

"To begin with, I will condense and review what I wrote in my first book about the twenty-first century. Uh, kkuh-hum.

"The twenty-first century is a study in the difficult task of reclaiming the hallowed values which make our human species and our civilization great. In the twentieth century, worldwide, our culture was in a tumultuous decline. Many men chose to allow themselves to believe the *peculiar* and *insane* idea that women are *people*, just as men are. They forgot the age-old wisdom that the human race is the Race of *Man*.

"Damn, here's the bot. Help me sit upright. Now let me put my arms—No. Uh . . . No! No . . . I can't . . . Let me down again. Carefully! I'll have to wait for one-gee to put on a shirt. Raise the cabin temperature ten degrees.

"Where was I? Okay.

"Religious men will say that Satan put his vile and

blasphemous words into the mouths of women, making some women, and weak men, believe that women—despite their *not* having been created in the masculine image of God—are *equal* human beings along with men. This contemptuous idea greatly weakened our culture, handing us over to the evils of the Devil. Sexual perverts gained prominence, to the obvious detriment of civilization.

"Damn, it's hot! Where's that bot?

"'I wanted you to raise the temperature ten degrees *Fahrenheit,* not centigrade, damnit! Ten degrees *Fahrenheit* from the temperature it was when I took off my shirt and first told you to raise the temperature. It's now damned hot. Centigrade is *too much!*'"

"Where was I? Oh, yeah.

"This may be a surprising fact to many men in the future, but there was a time when a very small minority of men — for reasons no sane man can begin to understand — gladly played the female sexual role with other men, and 'free' females pretended to have sex — sterile, non-reproductive sex — with one another, one of them using — presumably — a manufactured plastic substitute for the God-blessed male organ, a monstrous blasphemy. Those perverts were allowed to flaunt their sickening immorality in the faces of decent men and their families. Confusion reigned as the economy crumbled and the birthrate fell world-wide, all the fault of the Queers and those who tolerated them. It didn't have anything to do with what pussy-whipped Liberal men said: that the American president used genocide and *radioactive* ammunition to make war against small oil-rich countries in the Middle East and bring them into line with American need. And that *radioactivity* was the reason for the lowering sperm-count worldwide. . . .

No! Perverts contaminating the ethical standards of society were responsible for lowering sperm counts world-wide! Obviously.

"This is an important matter for all of us. Early members of my Family were involved in the American military, and one—*a colonel!*—was viciously killed by savage Arabs using stolen American equipment. Those Arabs were not-White."

"Back to the summary. Uhh. Kkhh. Kkhh. For the book.

"As we now *finally* understand, *women are nothing more than specialized human-like female animals, whose reason for existence is to provide sexual release for human men and to reproduce the human species, giving men sons* and incidentally also producing more females so the next generation of men can also reproduce and carry on the species.

"Any deviation from — or sick, sterile *imitation* of — this God-blessed reproductive behavior, *including the use of so-called 'birth-control' devices or pills*, was and **is** an insult to God and cannot be tolerated by any successful civilization.

"Surprisingly, but as sign of the sad degeneracy of those times in the twentieth century, a man using a woman for sexual release against *her* will — *as if a non-person, a human-like animal created by God to serve men, has a* real *will, like a person, a man, does* — was *illegal.* A man could be *jailed* for most of his life for the '*crime*' of using a woman or a nubile girl in the way God intended him to.

"And, in many places in the world, a woman could legally kill a *fetal-baby* a man had planted in her womb, just because *she* didn't want it! Monstrous! No female animal can be given the choice of whether or not to carry to term the seed of a male. *That is what the female is **for**.* Only men are fully human. Walking wombs are not people. They are **things**. Things for men to own and use.

"Even a cursory study of history will teach the average man that men and *men alone,* are the human species, and women are at best *accessories* to the life of men as we creatively *compete with one another to* **conquer** *the future.*

"The lowering population of the proletariat worldwide— losers who were all too stupid and incompetent to take advantage of the freedoms Capitalism gave them— produced a crisis for the Families, who needed Workers for the military, for agriculture, manufacturing, transport, personal servants, and so forth. Beginning at the mid-point of the twenty-first century, the Families were forced to develop our semi-sapient robots, to replace the dwindling population of Prole-Workers due to lowering sperm-counts and laws stupidly limiting the reproductive use of women. Bots proved to be much more reliable Workers than the Proles ever were. They don't need toilet or lunch breaks, sick leave, vacations, weekends, holidays, retirement pay, or even sleep. They never go on strike. They don't form unions. As *property*, rather than supposedly human '*employees*,' the bots don't need to be paid.

"*Proles*, as Workers, were not economically viable. The

ludicrous fantasy of *'democracy'* had to be enshrined in White, Western Civilization in nineteenth and twentieth century culture, *so the Proles would not suspect they were slaves.* The pretense of letting them vote to 'choose' which Family member would 'represent' them was ultimately found in the twenty-first century to be expensive and unnecessary. That whole farce of *'elections'* had always been a waste of time and money.

"The least educated Proles had been, for generations, limited to manual labor, either outside as agricultural Workers or inside in factories and mines as adjutants to machines. They were otherwise only suited as servers in junk-food restaurants, or as harshly supervised personal servants to leisured members of the Families.

They inevitably died of starvation after the bots replaced them. In addition, the Families were forced to shoot huge crowds of Proles for rioting outside the Domes protecting the Families' unspoiled, unpolluted lands. This culling of worthless Proles was a good thing, since they were no longer needed for work which was more easily, and much more cheaply, done by the bots.

"Then many of the Proles who survived the culling disappeared when large space ships crewed by squishy green aliens took many of them away from Earth.

"They were probably used as food. There couldn't have been any other use for them.

"Oh, and oddly enough, in the twentieth century, after their small children were grown, women from superior, Capitalist families briefly rose to prominence in business and politics, so that by the beginning of the twenty-first century, the traditional nuclear family — which had erroneously included the family womb as an adult member — had nearly been destroyed. Only a few scattered nuclear families staggered on, struggling to insert into government the basic morals of a society governed by God the Father, a stern and jealous God, *whose Bible was addressed only to men, for **only men** are His greatest creation. **Only men are people**.*

"Then, in 2082, a neo-Fundamentalist preacher, the Reverend Cletus A. Johnson, rose to power, usurping *the outmoded and **female-infested** electoral process*, bringing about a Theocracy in the USA — the glory of modern Dominion-Christianity — something which had long been desired by most right-thinking men.

"He and his many followers set a glorious example for their descendents. Their women—who were used solely for the sexual and reproductive necessities ordained by God—were not housed within the old-fashioned, out-moded, and degenerate '*nuclear-family*,' but were kept in separate, secure facilities, the femhouses, where they would never again fall prey to the insanity of considering themselves *equal* members of the Family of Man. Women of the Capitalist Families were prized so much as incubators that they were married as teenagers, to bear children "in sorrow and in pain" in the femhouses, while men could go about the male business of exploring as well as *competing for resources to exploit.*

"Thus, men and boys could live their lives free of the weakening influence of females and could set aside — away from business and the important activities of men — those *socially trivial occasions* when a man needed either to achieve a healthy sexual release or to reproduce by impregnating a suitable womb.

"Outside the Domes, in the worthless slum regions, the lower orders of Proles have now — at the dawn of the twenty-fourth century — not yet been completely eliminated as the worthless pests they are. The lower class used to call themselves 'the Working Class.' *As if there was any dignity at all in the kind of work the Proles did before bots were manufactured for those jobs.* Now, outside the Family Domes, somehow, a small, tattered remnant of Proles manages to scratch out a meager existence in a soup of foul air, filthy water, and contaminated soil. There are so few of them, they won't last long.

"Among those few Proles still living outside the family Domes, we hear they still maintain a twisted version of the nuclear-family. Women equal to loser-men! How *revolting* and unhealthy.

"What the Proles do, how they live, what perversions they tolerate, are now of no consequence to the UFE, the United Families of Earth, who control *all* the Earth in a vital and dynamic system of Free Enterprise. Capitalism is *obviously inevitable,* (like Gravity) — the most glorious pinnacle of human civilization.

"Those Proles who have managed to educate themselves to be useful to us in the UFE — in quasi-creative capacities as programmers of bots, and as repairers of delicate machinery — are privileged to live within the Civilized Zones, those Domed-over areas owned and controlled by one Family or another. They are required to give up their ersatz nuclear-family living, and put their females in upper-Prole femhouses in the Domes, separate from the Family Femhouses. Or if they insist on living with their women, they must live outside the Domes in the dangerous slums with all the useless Proles, who are now in a state of completely unorganized *anarkhy*, savages in chaos."

"Uh, I'm tired. Three gees is exhausting, and I must wait several hours to try again to keep food down when the ship returns to three gees after the one-gee break. I'm going to catch some more sleep."

*   *   *

"I woke up and ate as soon as the one-gee alarm sounded. Then I *'eliminated,'* and took a shower. My stomach feels better. Now I can really sleep."

"According to the Library, this spaceship doesn't look like the ones depicted on the lurid covers of SF magazines in the early twentieth century, with big rocket exhausts at the back end, and the front end pointed. This spaceship has some sort of exhaust-like things and oddly twisted metal at both ends: one end to accelerate, the other end to decelerate. And at each end of the ship there is a glob of water, in the form of ice, to absorb the shock of our hitting grains of interstellar dust at great speeds or to absorb radiation intensified by the extreme speed at which we hit it. As I understand, the ship needs to slow down once we get to Alpha Centauri, or we will zip past and go on into the rest of the galaxy at nearly the speed of light — 186 thousand-plus miles per *second* in a vacuum — which is *damned* fast.

"This ship moves through space by drawing energy from the quantum vacuum, an engineering secret we got from that derelict ship my triple-Great Uncle found. More scientific *gobble-de-goook* I can't pretend to understand. I tried studying the history of science one time, but it got *way* beyond me. So, I contented myself with studying how the advancement of science influenced what was possible in engineering, especially manufacturing and robotics, and how all that affected society as a whole. By society I mean the only part of the human race worth caring about, *the survivors, the evolutionary winners*; that is, specifically, *the Families*, the United Families of Earth.

"The only thing I need to know about the quantum vacuum is that it has the energy to drive our spaceships great distances out into the galaxy, so we don't have to carry tons of fuel. We can expand our markets and get even richer and more secure, and if the Darsen Family does it first, we will have a leg up on all the other Families, our only worthy adversaries in the noble competition of commerce.

"Now that we are free of that artificial Barrier the damned Galactics put around our solar system, the twenty-fourth century will be the century in which the best of the Race of Man shall go out into the galaxy and conquer it, take all its resources for our own, and discover earth-like planets to colonize with our superior seed. We will, with our bots, make those new planets fit for mammalian-Earth life, so we may safely transfer our food animals and our females there. Sex, sons, and steaks: these are the essentials of a full life for a Man.

"Eventually, maybe even in my lifetime, the Families

will be able to leave the rotting corpse of Earth behind. The careless greed of earlier centuries—and the pollution of air and water with early-manufacturing waste products—ruined the planet. When we—the Families, the winners, the superior breed, those humans who have proved to be *the fittest* — leave the Earth — the left-behinds, the Proles, the losers, can slide into extinction along with all the other inferior creatures of that weak, ailing planet we must discard —

"Woops! Freefall. I hope there's nothing wrong!

"The damned bots didn't bother to warn me, but I stayed strapped in my damned waterbed while the ship was in freefall. I didn't want to get hurt flying around the room—I mean, the cabin—when the acceleration came back without warning.

"So, I lay here, and the bed rolled around on a track I hadn't noticed before, until I was lying on what had been the "ceiling." Then, the deceleration started. First at one-gee, so I almost got up to eat, and then, with only a loud, short alarm-warning, to three-gees. I heard a nasty metallic crash when the ship went to three gees. I hope no irreplaceable bot broke.

"I'll have to get the bots to move the Library screen to the old "floor." I wonder if the ship's Library has a copy of <u>A Turning Point</u>?

"Zzzzzz-uh? One-gee? Where was the one-gee-warning-alarm? When? I was sleeping. How long? Do I have time to get up and eat and so forth?

"I'm hungry. I'm getting up."

"'Help! Bots! Help! Damnit. Help! Help! Hell-ll-ll-pp!'"

"'Uh. Pick me up. Gently! Put me in the waterbed.' Ow! Why the hell wasn't there a three gee warning-alarm?

"I guess my arm is only sprained, not broken. It would hurt a lot more if a bone broke.

"The sudden increase in acceleration—no, deceleration— at three gees drove me down onto the floor. The deck, rather. Good thing I've got bots to serve me, not Proles like in the twentieth and half the twenty-first century. The bots are stronger and hold up better at three gees.

"I better call for a repair-bot to fix the damned alarm system."

"I've got repair-bots to fix the quantum-vacuum drive. The QV-Drive they call it. I've got a repair-bot to fix the oxygen generating system, and repair-bots to fix several other systems including the microwave oven for my "gourmet" meals. But there is no repair-bot for the alarm-system. That crash I heard at turnover, when the ship began to decelerate, was both the alarm controls tied to the ship's clock *and* the bot which was programmed to fix them if they malfunctioned.

"Good thing I still have my watch. Ten hours to one-gee. A medbot gave me some pain pills. I've been sleeping a lot. The monotony is getting to me."

"The Library has a lot of twentieth-century movies on file. I'm sick of watching them. Women all over the place, walking freely in the streets and offices, interfering in the affairs of men, acting like *people*. Watching those films was no help in relieving my loneliness, as I am by now *trillion and trillions* of miles from home.

"Without being able to refresh myself with healthy male company, the stories in the movies were not just interesting examples of the strange degenerate culture in the twentieth century, interesting to me as an historical anthropologist. But instead, they made me feel alien in my own good male skin. *Romantic love!* What nonsense.

"I never thought I would miss the guys I used to eat with now and then in the cafeteria at the Darsen Apartments. What fun we had! Laughing. Horseplay. Planning our baseball and basketball tournaments. I wish to hell I was home. Damnit.

"This expedition better be worth it. If I survive, I'm going to buy a second wife. The one I have now, I admit, I'll just use to impregnate. Sex with her was never as much fun as I've heard sex can be. She was always stiff and unresponsive. Not even as much fun as the one time I used a hooker. Maybe I'll have earned enough status and be able to afford a third wife. Lots of sons. I want lots of sons! *Sex, sons, and steaks.*

"As soon as I graduated teen-school, I took my first consultant retainer-check, with the sign-on bonus, and attended the first wife-fair I could, that of the Zenke family. She was the prettiest one there, I thought. Better looking than her twin who stood beside her in the dock. The bidding for her was fierce, but a couple of my best buddies, cousins Delano and Warren, guys I had grown up with, staked me some extra money, and I finally won her. In return, after I paid them back, I promised to name the first two sons I got from her after them.

"Two years and she hasn't conceived yet. I guess I'll have to breed her more often when I get back to earth. Or my Family will have to sue the Zenke family for defective merchandise. Girls sold as wives are always guaranteed to be fertile.

"She was, of course, sired by a Zenke, from a Family my Family has had profitable business dealings with for generations. Even though a wife is only a semi-human animal designed for sex and reproduction, she *does* pass along the superior Family-genes of her Sire and the woman who bore her. So we get our wives from the other Families, even though they cost more than buying, or capturing, a pale Prole-female would.

"All the female babies born in our femhouses, sired by Darsen men, are of course the property of the Darsen Family. They are important commodities which bring in lots of money at wife-fairs. Most Families give a percentage of the sale price to the man who sired each female. That's why I took one of a pair of twins for my first wife, as my brothers also had, on the good advice of my father, because a female who is one of a pair of twins is much more likely to give birth to twins. More sons in a shorter length of time, out of one female, and more females to sell to other Families. My wife is so pretty. Prettier female offspring will sell more easily for more money.

"I have never been tempted to purchase a wife from the Proles. Many consider that a perversion, and in the Darsen Family, men of any age or status are not allowed to purchase either their first or second wife from outside the Families.

"Many think that if a very successful man, who already has more than one son, purchases a very light-skinned Prole for his third, fourth, or fifth wife, with her wild genes, this brings into the Family a possibly of hybrid vigor. A few men who were born of such wild-mothers have been very successful, or their sons have, and they have made very profitable contributions to their Families. I am descended from the wild fourth wife of my triple-great-grandfather who was his generation's CEO of the Family and was thus rich enough and of high enough status to have six wives. For variety, he purchased a very pretty wild woman, the pale-skinned, youngest female offspring of his best Prole programmer of semi-sapient-robots.

"Strangely, after giving him a son – who was soon taken away from her, of course, and suckled on goat's milk – she escaped from the femhouse in the middle of the night and ran to the slums outside the Domes. She was never found, although hunting parties, heavily armed Guards, were sent to capture her. They docked her father's pay, of course, for her price. He shouldn't have raised a female so rebellious she failed to be properly subservient, thinking she was a person. My triple-great-grandfather was furious. Since she was new, she had apparently still been his favorite. Family legend has it that she always fought him when he came to use her. Fighting, of course, makes the victory of coitus more fun, more exciting. Because females are weaker and always lose. As is proper. Praise the Lord.

"I believe our social system is best. More fair to the

females, not to push them to be what they are not and can never be. Those feminists in the twentieth century— unnatural females all, many of them perverts—injured more than just our society with their calls for 'equality' for females. They injured the females themselves. Poor things.

"Sons are *people* to carry a man's line and his name and his Family honor. Female babies are future incubators, walking-wombs, to be eventually sold to other Families for their medically supervised potential to produce healthy children of their superior class. Infertile females must serve as hookers — subject to the lash if they fail to satisfy their customers — that being the only other use to which a pretty young woman can be put. Older females, past childbearing age, serve as housekeepers in men's houses until they retire to the femhouses to uselessly soak up resources. Ugly female babies who grow up to be unattractive are housekeepers in the femhouses all their lives.

"Girl children who are potentially attractive enough to interest a normal man are raised in the femhouses, not in the home where their Sire lives, so there is no chance for a possibly weak-minded man to become fond of a "daughter" and forget she is not a person, as the Proles often do. After they are taken from their mothers, to be fed on goat's milk for a year, boys are raised in their father's house, by their fathers, untainted by females.

"God, I'm sleepy! And bored. I wonder when we'll get to Alpha-Centauri? I don't even have a viewscreen to see out of. Oh, well, I guess the bots know how to do all the space-navigation necessary. . . .

SHIP'S LOG ENDS. . . .

Starship Darsen decelerated steadily for several weeks more on its way to Alpha Centauri. Because the small alert light which should have told him so was burned out, Brad was unaware his recorder had stopped working. He compulsively talked and talked to the disk-corder and tried not to lose his grip on sanity. He was terribly lonely. The unfocused rage he felt towards his father grew until he had no energy to do further work on his second book.

*   *   *

ARRIVAL AT ALPHA CENTAURI

The best prole-engineer-programmers the Darsen family employed had programmed the navigation and steering bots. They had done their jobs with the complete competence expected of them.

Fortunately, Darsen family representatives had been to the Alpha Centauri system more than a century before to search for resources to exploit, before the galactics moved to exclude the competitive and hierarchical human species from the rest of the galaxy by erecting a Barrier englobing the Solar System between the Kuiper Belt and the globular Oort Cloud.

Alpha Centauri A and B orbit each other in elongated oval orbits at an average distance of 23AU, almost two billion miles apart. Alpha Centauri A, a G2 yellow star almost exactly like Sol, the sun of Earth, had three rocky airless planets like Mars orbiting within 2AU of the star's surface. None of them contained minerals in great enough concentrations near enough to the surface for bot-mining to be practical. Alpha Centauri B, a K1 orange star slightly dimmer and cooler than Sol or A, had one rocky airless planet in a stable orbit with an unexpectedly large deposit of gadolinium, a rare-*'earth'* metal, within three miles of the surface in one area. Darsen family bots had been mining and refining there for over a hundred years, stockpiling the gadolinium until a ship from Earth could come to collect it.

The century of waiting had not worried the bots. They communicated calmly with the navigation bots on Starship Darsen, sending them the exact location of the system's wormhole, and the exact speed and angle at which it must be entered in order to reach a certain star system with known earth-like planets. Brad, strapped in his waterbed in freefall, listened to the binary language of the bots on B's one planet talking to his ship-bots. He gritted his teeth against his nausea and hated his father even more. He was sure his sense of helplessness and the boredom would kill him soon.

THROUGH THE WORMHOLE

Without warning from the broken alarm system, the bots accelerated the ship at 3Gee to the area of the wormhole entrance and decelerated at 5Gee. Automatically, Brad's waterbed took a semi-circular route – from one "floor" up a "wall" to the other "floor" in freefall between acceleration and deceleration. Brad lost the contents of his stomach, mostly acid. Then in freefall again, using the lateral steering jets, the bots precessed the ship until it was pointed directly at the wormhole, and accelerated through it from two thousand, two hundred and sixty-three miles, three hundred and eight feet, eleven inches away, at 4.65871Gee. Overcome with nausea, Brad hardly noticed.

book three
A PLANET IN ANARKHY

*   *   *

After the ship decelerated on the other side of the wormhole, Brad heard the exchange of radio-talk between his bots and – to his uneasy surprise – *humans* on a space station over two hundred million miles away:

"grx'rrds Uukllrr'tss Chomsky, ♦ymsskk'll ^hhkst Kayoss. Hgg*tth ssss'st. This is Chomsky Station, in stationary orbit of planet Kayoss. Please respond."

"This is the bot-crewed starship, Darsen-1-C-97. We have a Darsen scion as passenger and consultant. We require a docking-port, immediately."

There was a pause of thirty-six minutes – due to radio waves being limited to the speed of light – and then the bot on the Darson- starship received: "Whoa! Where're you from?"

Another eighteen minutes, and the bot's reply was heard on Chomsky Station: "Darsen Manufacturing Facility #3, Ell-Four, registry at Verne City, Luna."

The comWorker on duty at the arrivals-radio said, loudly, "You're from Earth?"

Another comWorker kicked herself away from her workstation and rolled on her wheeled chair across the center space of the radio-room to the man at the arrivals-radio desk. "Hey, Bud. I've attended some Defense Syndic seminars about what to do if we ever receive visitors from Earth. So, let me have the mike."

"You're a smartass, Dana," Bud said, taking the radio-rig off his head and handing it to her. "Okay, I'll take the Kayoss-Up-radio. There's always more to do there anyway. I forgot to put a book in my com-pad today." He kicked himself in his wheeled chair back across the radio room to the station she had just deserted.

"Unknown ship. Unknown ship. Are you really from Earth?" Dana asked. "Over."

There was a long pause, while she entertained herself by reading part of a novel from her com-pad, and then the unknown ship answered: "This is the Starship Darsen, out of Verne City, Luna. We have a Darsen consultant aboard. Please provide docking data immediately. Do you copy? Over."

"Are you really a robot? she asked as soon as the starship's radio message reached her. "Over."

Pause of thirty-six minutes: "I am a bot. Are you a prole? Over."

"Ah! Yes, uh, I am a human being, a typical member of the proletariat. May I speak to your human consultant? Over."

Another pause of thirty-six minutes passed while Dana finished one chapter, started another, and waited for the bot's reply to reach her: "Please wait. I will see if the scion will speak with you. Over."

She waited patiently while the ship-bot radioed Dana's request to a bot in attendance on the human, who asked the human to speak to the prole on Chomsky Station, using the microphone plugged into the attendant-bot.

Brad Darsen thought about what he would say to a prole unexpectedly found out in space: "This is Bradley Darsen, consultant for the Darsen Family. Let me speak to your supervisor. Over." Brad wondered what Family had beaten the Darsens into space. How had they escaped the Barrier?

"Supervisor? Um, we have no such position. I am the senior comWorker in the Station radio-room right now. I'll have to do. Over."

Brad was instantly furious, but his quick reply was lost on Dana as she calmly read from her com-pad during the anticipated thirty-six minute round-trip pause before his reply reached her: "You are insubordinate," Brad snapped. "Let. Me. Speak. To. A. Family. Member. Now. Over." He spoke clearly and firmly. *What nerve! What Family out here has allowed their proles to run wild? And why was that guy on the radio speaking in a falsetto? Or was he a castrate?* The Families used castrates to "guard" the femhouses. No one had thought of any other use for them.

"In*subordinate?*" She laughed heartily into her microphone. "No one here is *subordinate* to anyone else. And we have no Families such as you would recognize. You'll have to speak to me. I have the most experience here to access your needs and solve any problem you might have. Over."

After another thirty-six minutes, she heard his reply: "Who's in charge? I demand to speak to whomever is in charge! Uh, over, damnit."

She sighed wearily. "That's me. Dana Goldman. I'm the

ah, supervisor, uh, "*in charge*" of this radio-link. How can I help you? Over."

Another thirty-six minute pause: "A Jew? How can you be a Jew? I thought we got rid of . . . Uh, kkuh, over."

"I'm not Jewish, although sometimes I wish I was. Now, we need to assign you a berth. Over."

She waited the thirty-six minutes, and then heard: "Do you revere the Word of our Lord? Over." He asked, although he was not very religious himself. Still, the forms had to be observed. Jesus was the glue that held civilization together, the god who blessed the glorious work of business, rewarding the virtuous with fortune. He had to make sure he wasn't talking to an *atheist.*

"I'm not going to talk with you about religion," Dana said. We are sending you a homing signal. Please follow it to your berth at the Station. Tell your … uh … bots. Someone will greet you when you arrive. Over." She leaned back in her chair, exhausted by the effort to communicate with someone who sounded like a madman.

His reply, after a few seconds less than the usual pause — he had interrupted and begun speaking before she had said, "Over." — took her by surprise: "No! I want to land on the planet," he shouted. "Damnit! Over, over!"

"There is no place on the planet you can safely land," she told him. "UFOs are not welcome. They can carry bio-material incompatible with Kayoss. And you must be immunized against our indigenous microscopic life. The medical stuff is essential. You will not be allowed to visit the planet without it. We are sorry. We will restrict your movements only a little, and only as absolutely necessary for our health and yours. Have your bots follow our laser signal. Coming at you right now. Over."

After the pause, he sounded a little more sane: "Well, I understand medical necessity. This all seems very irregular, but okay. Over."

"Someone will meet you when you dock. Chomsky Station out." She kicked herself in her wheeled-chair away from the arrivals-radio desk, saying, "Woo! Bud, Marsha, how about going flying with me in the Hub after work? I'm gonna need to unwind!"

"How the hell did they get through the Barrier?" Marsha mused.

Over the next several days, lateral steering thrusts and freefall mixed with varied acceleration during minute changes in direction made it impossible for Brad to keep any food down, and interrupted, without warning, any chances he took to shower or "eliminate." When the bots informed him that the ship was docked, he ate something even though the ship was in freefall, then "eliminated," and carefully read the directions on the oxy-mask which let him shower in freefall without drowning. Afterwards, he dressed in his best business suit, dark blue slacks and matching tunic with an old-fashioned tie-appliqué, and called for a bot to lead him to the airlock where he could disembark.

Coasting slowly in freefall through a transparent tube from his airlock to the Station let Brad catch a glimpse of the planet below. It looked rich and healthy, blue and white and slightly green and brown. *A find!* he gloated, forgetting for a second that there *had* to be another Family there already, or he would not be visiting a thriving civilization with a space station and medical '*stuff.*'

"Welcome to Chomsky Station." As Brad poked his head out of the transparent tube, a young man – with dark brown eyes, bright, curly strawberry hair matching his bushy mustache, wearing dark blue shorts and a green tee-shirt – smiled at the earthman. Having delivered his greeting, he held out his right hand towards Brad. In freefall, he floated out from a handle on a wall nearby, his knees bent. He was wearing socks the same color as his light-brown, healthy-tan skin.

Noting the man's skin colour, Brad decided he must be an outdoorsman, tanned from the sun, certainly not a common prole, for proles were never as pale as White people, and the Families were always composed of White people (except in Asia, because some pale-coloured Chink-Families had become wealthy in the early twenty-first century).

Well, the Family who had built the orbital station would not insult a member of another Family by sending anyone less than a Family Member to greet him, even though the young man with curly strawberry-red hair was dressed rather casually for escorting an important visitor. *I'll teach them how important I am!* Brad thought. He held onto the edge of the station's opening with his left hand, stretched out his right, and shook the other man's hand. "I'm Brad Darsen," he said.

"William Johnbrown. Again, welcome. Come this way, with me. You can pull yourself along with these handles on the bulkhead, see? Like this." He demonstrated, looking to Brad like a fat four-legged spider crawling along a wall.

"We have to put you in Quarantine for a little while. But don't worry. I'll stay with you to keep you company. Move slowly; the sense of gravity will increase as we go along. You're docked in freefall at the center of the station's rotation, at what we call the 'south pole.' We are headed outward and 'north' toward the living floor of the station. Maybe you saw, coming in, the station is shaped like a big spinning tin can. It's six miles in diameter."

"Well, Mr. Brown –" Brad said as he pulled himself along behind the light-brown-skinned man.

"Johnbrown."

"What? I thought it was William."

"My *last* name is Johnbrown. I was born and raised in the village of Johnbrown, on the island of Harper's Ferry. So I am a Johnbrown. We all have long last names, the people who were born in the various villages of Harper's Ferry Island. There's Osborne-Anderson, Annwoods, Sheildsgreen, Harriet-Tubman, Dangerfield-Newby, and so forth." He stopped at a round door in a wall facing them and pressed a large button to open it. "In here now, careful, there's about one tenth gee. The door is in the ceiling; we'll drift down to the floor. It's about twelve feet, not so far. About the same as jumping down two feet on Earth. That's it. We're in an airlock of the Q-Unit, quarantine, so we take off all our clothes. Put them in the chute here. They'll be decontaminated and washed. Close your eyes."

"Don't you have Families?" Brad asked as he was stepping out of his pants and underwear, clumsy in the low gravity with his eyes closed.

"Hold your breath! Of course we do. Everybody does!"

William shouted in the sudden storm-like conditions of the decontamination procedure as they were sprayed with a sharp-smelling liquid and the air in the airlock was rapidly exchanged "What does that have to do with anything?"

Brad's tie-appliqué had un-stuck itself from his tunic and wrapped itself around his head. He clawed it off his face. He opened his eyes to a squint. The other man was muscular, with a flat belly, in good shape, and … circumcised! … which was not normal, as far as Brad was concerned. That was how the Jews mutilated their God-given dicks and *the man couldn't be Jewish, could he? Not with blonde hair*, he thought. Brad realized, uncomfortably, he hadn't been completely naked in the presence of another man since gym class in teen-school. Nakedness for a grown man was for sex with a woman. "What is your *Family* name?" he asked, taking off his soaked tunic and bedraggled tie-appliqué and putting them in the chute. He was irritated, dripping from the strange disinfectant-chemical and shivering in the lingering wind.

"Oh, you mean that old-fashioned patriarchal stuff, from Earth before the Migration? We don't do that any more," William said.

Brad stood, naked, in a corner, using his elbows against the walls to push his feet against the floor in the light gee-field, as far from the other naked man as space in the airlock would allow. "What? Migration?"

"You know, before the Galactics — it was the Geejjikk, actually — before they set up the Barrier to keep the … uh, Imperialist … uh, Capitalist … humans out of the rest of the galaxy. The Geejjikk came to Earth in vast ships and took away huge numbers of the proletariat out of the slums all over the globe, once they determined that the culture of the humans living on the open Earth between the Families' Domes had evolved past a competitive, hierarchical economic system to a peaceful, non-hierarchical, co-operative world-wide society."

"No. The proles are in a state of ***anarkhy***," William said.

"Precisely. My ancestors, about a hundred years ago, entered the alien starships because they wanted a better life for themselves and their children, better than living on Earth where they had to put all their collective energy into simple survival with very little left over for mending the damaged, near-catastrophic environment. They wanted a better way of life, and healthy grandchildren, with a realistic expectation of long-term survival for the human species on a planet where life was *not* just about to become extinct."

Brad stood rigid against the wall. *They locked us out of the galaxy because we're Capitalists? h*e thought. *Why? . . . They must have been afraid of us, of our competitive vitality!* "Uh," he said to the other man, "we thought those ugly, squishy aliens were taking our proles away to put in zoos, or to eat, or something. What you're telling me is very strange."

"There's the green light. That rectangular door beside you, there on your left. Go on in," William Johnbrown told Brad. *"Our proles?"* William thought, *Huh! I wonder what it's going to mean for us, to have the Bourgeoisie free in the galaxy? With their possessive attitudes ... their need to dominate ... their interest only in their filthy profits. . .*

"Here, Brad, take a robe," William said. "We don't have

to stand around in the nude. . . . Ah. . . . Doc." William addressed a man with dark brown skin colour in a face mask and a spotless white lab coat which floated gently around his trousers in the low gravity. "This guy here, Brad Darsen, is straight from old Earth, no other decontamination procedures yet, I believe. Right?" he asked Brad.

"No, no decontamination procedures so far," Brad answered. "I have no communicable diseases, not even a cold. We have pretty good health care, in the Family Domes on Earth. We've pretty well licked the common cold," he said, smiling faintly. "The Families are very civilized. I'm clean." He thought to himself: *A dark-prole. Damn! Don't they have any medbots? What the hell is going on?*

"I'm Doctor Vladimir Mikhail. I'm sure you're a clean person, Brad –"

"Mister Darsen."

"Ah," said the doctor, peering carefully at Brad's face. "In that case, *I* am *Doctor Mikhail* to you, not Doc or Vlad, as I would be to someone who automatically regards us as equals. I think you are going to find our society very strange, *Mister* Darsen."

Brad looked at the strangely – to his eyes, *savagely* — dark face of the doctor, and averting his eyes, said, "I'm sure you're right." *I just have to get through this decontamination nonsense, so I can get down to the planet and tally up the resources. The Family which has colonized this star system must be too sloppy to be able to hold it against the Darsen Family assault-bots Dad sent after me. They'll be waiting at Alpha Centauri. First our bots secure the planet, and then I can go home, to a new wife! Or two!*

Damn you, Dad, you thought I was expendable! I'll show you. I'll bring the Darsen Family the ticket to more wealth than any other man in three hundred years!

"We will need to analyze all your cells and your body fluids, Mister Darsen," the Doctor said. "Who knows what micro-organisms have arisen on Earth — in that filthy, dangerous environment — in over a hundred years that you are immune to, and carrying, which could easily kill any of us. We have to protect our biosphere. And you yourself will need to be immunized against having an allergic reaction to the great variety of microscopic proteins in the air and water of Kayoss."

"Okay," Brad said. "Send in the medbots."

"We have no medbots, Mister Darsen, not as you have on Earth. We use well-established Galactic nanobot technology. Come over here." The prole-doctor stood by a large machine which looked like a blocky metal bathtub filled with pinkish-green, soft gelatin. "Please take off your robe and climb in."

Brad tossed the dark-prole his robe, casually establishing in his own mind the servant status of the darkie-'*doctor*,' and climbed into the 'bathtub' filled with incomprehensible goop. He found it was deeper than he thought. Sitting down, the goop came up to his neck, and only his head was above the stuff.

The doctor bent to open a panel and press a few buttons. "We'll take a look at your general health, Mister Darsen, while we search for microorganisms and mutant prions you may be carrying which would be detrimental to us and to our planet's biosphere. Now, slide under the surface of the nano-medium, and take a deep breath."

"What, uh....."

"You won't drown. You see the medium is foamy? That's oxygen. William," the doctor said, catching his eye. "You can help. Please."

"So, what do you want for supper?" William asked, smiling at Brad, trying to put him at ease.

"What?"

"Supper. We have a suite here, while you're in quarantine and I'm keeping you company. Since you're busy right now, being analyzed, I'll make supper. You can make breakfast. Fair?"

"I can't cook. I never have."

"I'll show you tomorrow morning. Meanwhile, tonight, I was thinking something Alfredo? with pasta."

"Oh. Sure! Great."

"Chicken, rabbit, tuna fish or goat?"

"What?" Brad asked.

"You folks in the Earth-Domes, you eat meat, don't you?"

"Oh! Yes."

"Well, so do we. Ours is grown in vats, so we don't have to kill our animals. It's bad karma, you know, killing animals for food.

"Chicken, rabbit, tuna fish or goat," Willian continued. "That's what's available on Station right now. The Vat Collectives are all saving up their turkey for Thanksgiving. It's Tradition."

"Vats?"

"Sure. We grow animal protein in vats. I've done the work.

Simple enough. It tastes okay. We have no slaughterhouses. No matter how so-called 'humane' it is, killing is *killing.* So we can be good friends with our animals."

"How about beef?"

"No beef. Cows didn't make it on board the Geejjikk's rescue ships. Too large, and we really needed goats, because goat's milk is best for babies when their birth-mothers don't have enough. And goats eat ten percent less, I think, than cows, while producing something like twenty-five percent more milk."

Brad sat up straighter in the diagnostic tub and self-righteously lectured: "You can't let milk-less mothers ever breed again, or their girl-babies live. Or in a few generations, you'll have flocks of mothers who can't nurse at all. Bad for the species. Your Ruling-Family should know better."

"Hmm," William said, as he rechecked the settings on the side of the diagnostic tub. "I can see that *women,* and *reproduction,* are two subjects you and I must avoid, in the interests of serenity. Under you go." He quickly pushed Brad's head under the nano-medium, and held him under while the earthman trashed about, trying to escape, until Brad convulsively took a deep breath of the foamy medium, and suddenly calmed by its sleep-inducing properties, slid further down into the diagnostic *'bathtub.'*

William wiggled his bushy moustache, smirking. "Damn, I'm skilled," he said to himself. "So, here comes the Doc back to oversee the diagnostic process," he continued in a tone loud enough for Brad to hear. "I will now retire to the kitchen of our suite, to cook. I'll surprise you with the meat." He patted the side of the diagnostic tank in a friendly, absent-minded sort of way, smiling at Brad, who was already asleep, oblivious, and then William turned and left the room.

*   *   *

Brad never became accustomed to all the dark-skinned proles who worked in the Quarantine Unit. His feelings were mixed when he finally understood that William was not entirely a White person, and also not a scion of a Family. So there was no other Family in the star-system! The way was clear for the Darsen Family to move in! He would return to Earth a **winner!** His income, as discoverer, and owner, of enormous resources for the Family, would rise precipitously. He would be rich!

On the other hand, he felt insulted that proles of all colors in the Station Quarantine Unit treated him as though he were their *equal.* An equal of *Proles!* Who had, all of them, over the course of human history, proved themselves to be losers, *incapable* of succeeding in a vibrant Capitalist economy. Proles had always been incapable of doing anything but selling their labor to the winners in order to survive. Bots were better workers. There was no need for most proles to be allowed to live. They weren't useful.

While in the Q-Unit, Brad never learned to cook. William was very patient at first, explaining everything carefully, but Brad found the whole procedure so boring, he never really listened, and William soon gave up, doing all the cooking for both of them in their suite in the Q-Unit. Brad had to serve *himself,* however, right out of the *hot* pans on the stove! And he did have to learn to make sandwiches, which William would not do for him because no *cooking* was involved.

During that quarantine time, Brad was immunized against everything. He spent most of his time in the Q-Unit sick, feverish, or nauseated from the dermal-spray-injections he had been given. He slept whenever he could. William occasionally tried to engage him in conversation, to prepare him for the Anarkhist society he would be entering when they left Quarantine, but Brad could not concentrate on anything other than his own personal misery.

Two weeks before he was to be released and allowed to go down to the surface of Kayoss, the planet, Brad was put into a Healing-Pod, similar to the diagnostic tank, where special nanobots – made from his own proteins and iron – would sort through his body's vital systems and repair them: refolding proteins, replacing shortened or missing telomeres, unclogging arteries, destroying the occasional alien virus, dumping atoms of heavy metals, and removing any cancerous cells or mutant prions. "The Pods are a technology we were given when we joined the galaxy-wide civilization," William told him. "All art, science, and technology are shared among all the galactic species, you understand. We Humans spend time in a pod once an earth-decade, starting at the earth-age of thirty. Improves the life span. We still have a few of the original elders living among us who were born on Earth, more than a hundred earth-years ago."

"If that's true, I'd like to meet one of them," Brad said

as he settled naked and freshly scrubbed into the warm pinkish-green goo of the Pod.

"I read an article recently which said they have all gone star-traveling, on a special great starship with various realms at different temperatures, pressures, G-forces, and atmospheres. They'll be able to interact with many different species as they travel, and get to visit lots of different star-systems. The best way to avoid boredom when you're real old, I guess. Of course, we get to visit with other species right here on our own planet. There's a geodesic dome of chlorine-breathing Ttiiffsts next to the human villages of Mikhail and Bakunin which I hope to visit with you once you're out of the Pod and we can take the Skyhook down to Kayoss. Slide your head under the goo. You can do it this time without bring tricked, I'm sure. Good. Now, take that deep breath," William continued in a louder tone. "I'll set up some educational films for you to watch once we close the lid. You know you're perfectly safe. Just relax."

Brad had long since come to trust the calm, useful nature of the proles and the med-procedures he had encountered in the Q-Unit. He almost believed the proles were human. Sort of.

He was used to discounting proles as potential rivals. If they were typical of their whole strange culture, without even one Family to dominate and lead them, he had nothing but sad contempt for them. They would be pushovers for the leadership and exploitation of the Darsen Family. If they would so casually *give away a technology of life extension*, they were all damned fools, not suited to survive in a dangerous universe. Brad did not doubt the Universal Truth that survival *anywhere* demanded the strength, aggression and competitive edge of a truly superior species in order to prosper and dominate. And he knew the Families, especially his own — who were the peak of human evolution — to be strong enough, clever enough, and ruthless enough to win in every encounter with the damned squishy aliens of the galaxy.

For two weeks he floated in a fizzy pinkish cloud and watched educational films which filled him in on the environment and culture of the leaderless proles of Kayoss as well as its star-system.

Xye'tsst was a triple-star-system, with two earth-like planets, each circling a star of spectral type G2, very similar to Sol, the star of Earth. The third star was a red giant around which the other two stars orbited at 65AU and 59AU, respectively. The red star — for some reason called Marx by the proles — could be seen in the sky of Kayoss as a bright red dot day or night, except when it was directly behind the star Kayoss orbited. The sun of Kayoss was called Che. It orbited the giant red sun at 65AU.

The other nearly identical G2 star in the system, which orbited Marx at 59AU, was called Fidel. It could usually be seen in the sky of Kayoss at late dusk or early dawn, even through a thin cloud cover. The earth-like planet in orbit around Fidel was Nueva Cuba. It was also inhabited mostly, but not exclusively, by humans.

Spanish was the global language of Nueva Cuba, rather than English, as on Kayoss. Humans of both planets also spoke standard-panGalactic, almost from birth. And each human village had its own special language, its ***villang***, taught to very young children, who grew up trilingual, speaking English (or Spanish), the galaxy-wide panGalactic language, and the ***villang*** of the village in which they were born.

The triple-star system had been named Xye'tsst by the Geejjikk who had originally surveyed it, and the humans had not changed the system's name in their records, "out of respect and gratitude," the film's narrator said, "for the galactic community which had given the exhausted beggars from Earth their new homes."

Beggars! Brad thought angrily. *Good thing for those aliens they didn't pick up anyone from the Families. My ancestors would never have humiliated themselves by <u>begging</u> for space in the galaxy. Winners <u>take</u> what they want. They would never have begged for <u>anything</u> from those damned squishy aliens!*

The educational films continued. Oddly enough, or so Brad thought, the humans of Kayoss were organized into villages, not into families of any sort. They took their last names from the villages of their birth and childhood, not from the man who had sired them. They had no discernible government. It was insane Anarkhy. Women were apparently equal to men within the culture, which Brad thought was both ridiculous and unrealistic. In his opinion, the humans — proles, all of them, just working-class losers — were being allowed by the galactic aliens to *play* at being civilized. *They must be like <u>pets</u> to the aliens, taken care of like cattle. Maybe they are even, secretly, food. The Darsen*

Family will repair this insult once we take over! Damned squishy <u>things</u> making humans into pets! This insulting use of human beings, even inferior ones, will be stopped! When I am Viceroy, the only humans on the planet will be the Families with their loyally-programmed bots, and a few pale-skinned high-level proles to program, clean, and repair the bots. We will get rid of all those low-level darkie-proles the damned aliens have made into <u>pets</u>!

Since Brad had no apparent interest in visiting the living floor of the interior world of Chomsky Station, and since he was obviously very anxious to reach the surface of Kayoss, William Johnbrown took him directly from the Healing Pod to the Skyhook. Brad wore his own clothes – which had been decontaminated and cleaned for him – light-wool, pinstriped, dark-blue trousers with a matching tunic and a tie-appliqué, with hard shiny-leather shoes. William wore light blue cotton trousers, a darker green t-shirt sporting a large golden sun-like design on the front, and dark-blue canvas shoes.

A few obviously older people and one with a cast on one leg had taken the "civilized" seating at one end of the Skyhook car, and everyone else – all with skin significantly darker than the pale beige of White people – sprawled haphazardly on the soft, thick carpet, leaning against large pillows, their luggage, or each other. All the other proles were dressed much as William was, in varying colors and t-shirt designs. Brad noticed he himself was the only man wearing clothes which marked him as a successful man of business. Half the proles were apparently females, dressed just as the men were, the presence of breasts obvious under their t-shirts. *Are all the men eunuchs? Why aren't any of them sexually excited to be in the presence of so many females?* Brad thought. He put the nearly empty backpack William had given him over his crotch to hide his healthy but inconvenient erection.

Three aliens – looking to Brad like scarlet barrel-cacti with numerous shiny tentacles writhing around and over them – sat (stood?) in the middle of the car in the midst of several humans who were grinning at them.

There was a moment of freefall as the car started down the cable toward the surface of Kayoss. "Don't try to fly," William advised Brad, clutching his arm. "The speed of our descent will even out in a moment and anyone flying will fall with an acceleration of zero-point-nine-seven-seven-six earth-gees, the gee force of Kayoss." The car slowed and Brad felt his weight come back. He had been in and out of so many gee fields since his "adventure" had begun, he could not really tell he weighed slightly less than ninety-eight percent of what he would have weighed on Earth.

As the speed of their descent stabilized, a prole popped up and addressed the other passengers in the car: "Greetings fellow travelers. I am Angie Tubman." She was tall and thin, with a short kinky haircut, brown skin, an extremely handsome face with few lines, a smooth, unlined neck, and was apparently flat-chested.

Brad had not thought she was a female. *So, ugly females are allowed to live!* he thought. *Strange.*

"I am eighty-one earth-years old," the amazingly young-looking ugly-female continued, "the first baby born on

Berkman Island, and I've been living in Chomsky Station for the last fifteen years, working as an agronomist. I bring to share" – she held up a net bag filled with red globes – "tomatoes from my private garden. So sweet you won't even need salt. Who's next?" She sat down to enthusiastic clapping.

One of the scarlet cacti waved all its tentacles above its – (head?) – and spoke in what Brad assumed was standard-panGalactic, full of whistles. Balanced on the tips of its tentacles was a short stack of thin, flat, foot-and-a-half-foot purple-squares. The proles cheered.

Another human stood up, announced his name, age, and occupation (cook), and offered fresh-baked whole-grain bread from "the Chomsky Third-Village Kitchen Collective." Dramatically whipping out a saw-toothed bread-knife from a sheath on his belt, he began slicing the bread.

Others offered humus, mayonnaise, several kinds of crispy lettuce, peanut butter, and even salt. William offered up a gallon jug of fruit juice. Brad hadn't even noticed he was carrying the jug. Proles began making sandwiches, passing them out to those sitting by the walls, and to the elders in the "civilized" seats.

A stranger passed Brad a sandwich. It seemed to have some of the purplish stuff in it, along with humus, lettuce, and slices of tomato. He tried to pass the sandwich to William, who held up his hands and shook his head, indicating he had a sandwich of his own. He mumbled around the food in his mouth, "Try it. All humans like it."

Brad nibbled tentatively at his sandwich. The tomato was

very good, with more flavor than any tomato he had ever eaten. The humus was almost meaty in strength, and the purplish stuff was crunchy and had a strange yet succulent flavor which blended well with the rest of the sandwich. He ate it all, relishing the experience, and licked his fingers, looking around for more.

William clapped him heartily on the shoulder. It felt as friendly and as manly to Brad as fooling around with his baseball and basketball buddies in the Darsen House cafeteria on Earth.

"Good, huh?" William asked.

"Yes, it was," Brad answered, a note of confused wonder in his voice.

"There's a collapsible plastic cup in the backpack I gave you," William said. "Have some kiwi juice." He had the gallon jug slung over his right shoulder, controlling the angle of his pouring with his elbow. He handed a full cup to a short female prole with light brown skin, large breasts and curly red hair, and then put down the jug to twist the collapsed cup Brad gave him until it was securely useable. He resumed pouring juice for Brad and others who came over to him. Several cups later, he went to the proles in the "civilized" seats and gave them some juice.

Brad concluded he had no chance of getting a second sandwich, and actually, he realized, he was mostly full. "What was that purplish stuff?" he asked William when he came back, his jug almost empty.

"Hkkk⏛ttt," William answered.

"It came from the aliens, those scarlet barrels, didn't it? I mean, what is it made of?" Brad asked.

"We're not sure –"

"What?" Brad asked loudly. Other humans around them looked at him, surprised.

"Shh, don't yell," William said. "I mean we humans don't know how the Djuiivv make the hkk⍦ttt, but we know it is from one of their native animals – they say without harming the animal – and that it has proven to be harmless to humans – harmless but very tasty. It's a protein-cellulose blend, much like the Djuiivv themselves. The Djuiivv always bring hkkk⍦ttt to share when they travel. We're always glad to see them."

"The people running the Skyhook don't provide food for their passengers?"

"No. Transport Collectives provide only water – see that tank strapped over in the corner there? – as well as pillows, books, magazines, and toilet facilities. Traveling is always a chance to share food with other people. Sometimes what you get is very familiar, sometimes wonderfully different. I'll bet you'll be glad of a chance to eat hkkk⍦ttt again, won't you?"

"Oh, sure. Uh, how long is the trip down?"

"A little more than thirty-four hours."

"Won't we get bored?"

"Read a book. They're stacked over by the water tank. I already picked up a good historical novel for you, based on real events, about the early settlers on Nueva Cuba. Okay?"

"Yes, thanks." Brad reflected to himself that William seemed like a regular buddy to him sometimes, like a Family man, not like a prole at all.

Someone strummed a guitar, and the proles around them began singing:

"I'm the son of a sailor, and the sea's in my blood.
I love bellbottom trousers and a deck I can scrub.

I'd give my horse and saddle for a boat that will float.

'Stead of sailing a schooner, I've been milking a goat.

Yo, ho, ho, and a bottle of rum. Let me go where m' father's from. . . ."

The Djuiivv — happily breathing in exhaled CO_2 from the humans close around them — provided a counterpoint accompaniment which sounded strangely like three high boson's whistles enriching the old sea chantey.

Brad leaned back against a large pillow, folded his hands over his satisfied stomach, and smiled as he listened. Music always said a lot about a culture and its history. Of course, he believed only the last hundred earth-years or so of this extra-solar society's history were unknown to him. But he had never heard that particular song before. Everyone but Brad appeared to be singing.

Content after his sandwich, the man from Earth was willing to consider that these alien-affiliated proles were not as much disgusting and animal-like as the dirty slum-proles back on Earth. Still inferior, of course.

ON THE SURFACE OF KAYOSS

"You should leave that book here in the car, so other passengers can read it," William told Brad as they were about to disembark the Skyhook car.

"I haven't finished reading it yet," Brad complained.

"Memorize the title and leave it," William said. "It belongs with the Skyhook. You can look it up on any comunit, and print out your own copy if you don't want to read it off the screen. Come on."

Feeling like a prole beast-of-burden, Brad wore the small backpack William had given him. It contained his folded tunic; a change of clothes he had been given, similar to what William was wearing; the collapsible cup; and the sandwich of hkkk⏛ttt, peanut butter, and lettuce wrapped in a cloth napkin he had been given for breakfast. He was saving the sandwich for his lunch. All he wanted for breakfast was coffee. He had had no coffee in over two weeks, since before he had gone into the healing-pod. He could think of little else but coffee, coffee, coffee.

They stepped out of the Skyhook car into a wide echoing room with a high ceiling. Tall windows above the exterior doors they were facing flooded the arrivals-hall with sunlight. It seemed to be a warm summer's day. Proles of various skin colours came in from the bright sunlight and rushed past them, hurrying to board the Skyhook to go up-orbit.

"As you can see by the position of Che, our sun, high in the sky to the west, it is early afternoon down here,"

William said. "We're in Mikhail. It's a nice village. Let's look for a room in an inn."

"Coffee?" Brad asked.

"The inn where we find a room will have coffee. Come on," William answered

The two men exited the arrivals-hall onto a wide plaza with a sparkling fountain approximately in the middle. The blazing tropical sun made Brad's eyes water.

Children of both genders played in the marble bowl of the fountain beneath the falling water. Brad assumed some of the children were girls because they had longer hair than the others. Then he noticed all the children were naked, and some of the longhaired children were boys, whereas some of the shorthaired children were girls. *Boys and girls playing together! Naked!* Stunned, Brad stopped walking, undone by culture shock and moral disgust.

Concerned, William looked around for him, came back and took his arm, leading him down a brick-floored path past stone buildings with wide porches fronting on the path. "Okay, this one has a vacancy. You all right? Let's go in."

They signed in and walked up two flights of stairs – there was apparently no elevator – and found the room they were assigned near the end of a long hall. The view out the room's one dormer-window was over several rooftops to a yellowish glass wall divided into triangles by metal bars; the wall stretched wide and high into the sky, blocking off any other view.

"Uh. Lousy view. Couldn't we have made a reservation?" Brad asked.

"No. It's first come, first served," William answered.

"People can't always fulfill reservations, and they often forget to call and cancel. So, when I was twenty earth-years old — *sigh* . . . so long ago — we got together in our villages and our Work-groups and decided collectively not to allow reservations, except for people who have to travel to give a seminar or something similar."

"Who decided?"

"We all did, collectively, after ... oh, such long, *long* speeches and frenzied arguments and heated discussions. It came to be nearly eighty percent for doing away with vacation reservations, anything other than work-related travel, if I remember rightly. The Innkeepers' General Coordinating Syndic has the exact records, I believe. Well, let's go down to the inn's dining room and get you that coffee you seem to need so badly. And I admit I would like some too."

"Great, I'll bring my sandwich. It's past time for lunch."

"Can we share the sandwich?" William asked.

"Uh ... Uh, okay," Brad grumbled. "I guess so. You've been a pal."

"Good for you. You might be getting the hang of it." William skipped ahead down the stairs to the second floor.

"Hang of what?" Brad raised his voice as he hurried down the stairs after William and saw him turn the corner onto the last flight down.

"Egalitarian communism, on a personal level," William answered as he waited for Brad at the bottom of the last flight.

"Hell, that's how you do things here, isn't it?" Brad asked. "And I didn't pay money for the sandwich, so it isn't really *mine*... Can we get hkkk‑ttt down here?" Brad stumbled over the consonant-rich word and the odd internal buzz, but William understood him.

"Nope. Only when we travel and a trio of Djuiivv is along. Come-on over here." Standing in an open doorway, William beckoned. It was mid-afternoon. The dining room was empty.

Once they were seated with coffee they had fetched for themselves from the kitchen, along with a sharp bread-knife to split the sandwich, Brad asked, "Don't you have a government to decide things?

"Nope. Not a government as you would understand it. No elected *representatives* to serve as an executive committee for our society; no legislature to pass laws, to regulate by force the exchange of goods and services. . . . We regulate ourselves, cooperatively, without threats of violence, in agreements among work groups, open village meetings, and individuals," William said as he divided the sandwich. "Okay, I cut, so you choose."

Brad picked the half he thought was infinitesimally larger and maybe had more hkkk‑ttt in it, and said, "No government? That's chaos*! Anarkhy!*"

"Yep. Anarkhy. We *are* free. The name we gave our planet is a play on words. As if "Kayoss" is a synonym for anarkhy, which it is <u>not</u>. That definition is based on the outmoded idea that 'it is chaos when no *one* is in charge.'"

"But ... but ... How do you prevent a strong man becoming a dictator?"

"He couldn't do it alone. He'd need an army to conquer us and patrol us to keep us enslaved. People with an anarkhist philosophy as their basic belief system cannot be made into a conquering army, let alone an effective army of occupation. As a society, as an Anarkhist people, we have no 'habit of obedience,' as one long ago Earth-philosopher put it. A free person obeys nothing except hir own conscience."

"Her conscience? What the hell?"

"Not "her" —"*hihr*" – aych-*eye*-ahrr. Hir: a gender-free possessive pronoun, a combination of "his" and "her."

"Oh … well … what about crime? What about murder? Is murder not against the law?"

"Nothing is against the law. We have no laws, only customs. Laws never prevent crime. Look how many murders were committed down through Earth's history in places where murder was against the law. Look how many times the laws were twisted so that some people could commit murder when others could not. Capital Punishment, for instance, was clearly murder, especially once it was proven that, on average, at least twenty-five percent of those executed were innocent of the crime. Executions were a legitimized way to commit murder."

"But if nothing is against the law, what keeps people from stealing and killing willy-nilly? What keeps society together?"

"Think about it. Historically, many murders, or most thefts for that matter, were committed for money. We use no money, nor any equivalent medium of exchange. Food is free. Also housing, clothing, education, health care . . ."

"Well, what about serial killers, who kill for the fun of it, over and over until they are caught?"

"Most of the *victims* of serial killers were *women,* is that not so?" William asked. "*Misogyny* — the *hatred* of women — was the main motivating factor, was it not? The society of the twenty-first century on Earth, and centuries before, was thick with misogyny, wasn't it? And serial killers were usually found to be men who had problems with their sexuality, and blamed women for it. Women, who had everything most men needed to achieve a good sex life. Women, who withheld their — '*pussy*?' Was that the word? — from the man who needed it. Women who made him feel weak and impoverished sexually. Women, sexist men believed, had power over men, because of men's sexual *need*, and used that power to manipulate and victimize men. Right?"

"William, I can tell from what I've seen of your society – you proles do *not* understand: Women are animals. Not people –"

"Oh, Brad, I'm sorry. *Women* and *reproduction,* remember? We need to avoid those two subjects, if we are to have a harmonious relationship while you are visiting us."

"This supposed *prole-Utopia* you have built, with no Family to teach and guide you—"

"Really, Brad. We need to find another topic for discussion —"

"I've been so sick from the immunizations for so long, I haven't had a chance to observe and learn about your world. . . ." *I've got to get into their information systems. Find out what the material resources of this planet are,* Brad thought, choosing to forget the discussion about women. *Women!* When he was Viceroy, after the Darsen assault-bots had subdued the planet —and how easy it would be to dominate this planet and its naïve, childish inhabitants! — the problem of women would be solved once they were all locked into femhouses. *Hatred of women! Ha!* Once females were in their proper place, there would be no problem with women, no reason for sane men to hate them. That solution had worked on Earth, and it would certainly work on Kayoss. Brad knew he himself had never hated women. He had no reason to.

"William, how about if I take the rest of the afternoon to explore on my own?" Brad asked, suddenly determined to begin his survey of planetary resources. "This is the first chance I've had, and there must be people you want to see, without me hanging on your neck. Why don't we separate 'til this evening, let tempers cool, then meet for dinner and talk of something other than women and sex?"

"Good idea," William agreed. "But you have to promise me you won't lecture people about what you think is wrong with us. Okay?"

"Okay."

The two men left the inn together, Brad made a note of the name of the place, and they walked off in opposite directions. William went to a kemmerhouse — so named to honor the anarkhist-woman-writer who had invented the idea — to indulge himself in a little healthy and harmless commitment-free sex with a few like-minded acquaintances and strangers. And Brad went to the nearest public library – which he found by asking directions from the first pale-skinned man he saw – to use a comunit to hopefully ferret out the information he needed on the planet's resources, so he could estimate how *rich!* he was going to be after the Conquest of Kayoss.

They met back at their inn for supper. Brad briefly hung around outside the dining room, uncomfortable, uncertain what to do. William took him in to the food line, where they could chose their meal from the steam tables, served by kitchen Workers who smiled and talked to the diners as though many of them were old friends:

"Hey Rod, remember me? Francis. What'll you have? How's that talented kid of yours?"

"The goat steak, Francis. Oh, Peter is doing great, so his mothers tell me. One of his photographs won a teen-competition on Emma-and-Sasha Island, and will be published by the Annual Picturebook Collective on Machno Island next month. Thanks."

The next person in line said, "Chicken, Francis, and lots of potatoes, no peas. Move along then, proud papa. You're holding up the line."

"Okay, Rod; I'll see you at the meeting next week," the kitchen Worker called-out as the proud papa went to sit down.

"Brad, try the stir-fried chicken and veggies," William said quietly in an aside. "The sauce is fabulous; it's a standard recipe. Take some rice too."

When the two men were seated at a small table along one wall, Brad found William's suggestion to be delicious, and he ate quickly, so he wouldn't have to share any of it. "Woo! Better cooking than our bots in the Family Domes can do, that's for sure," he said, pushing his plate away, leaning back, and sipping his coffee.

"I thank you, on behalf of the entire human race," William said, grinning.

"What's on the agenda this evening?" Brad asked.

"Well, this is the friendly Village of Mikhail: root, as they say, of the Skyhook. So, nearly every evening, there's a sort-of-party in the town square. A good place to see and be seen. They have so many visitors, you know, because of the Skyhook; the evening circle-stroll is a good place to find townspeople and travelers you might know. I'll pick up an evening-picnic-pack as we're leaving."

"Uh, Okay."

The sun had set and the evening was warm and summery. Brad noticed — as they walked together toward the village square along a brick path lighted with yellowish pole-lights above — that there was very little use of neon signs, and a paucity of shops offering interesting goods for sale *No. They would be giving things away, wouldn't they?* he thought, disgusted. The lack of bustling commerce and gaudy competition between businesses seemed dull to him. *I wonder what the cities are like?* he thought. He asked William about cities.

"We haven't any cities, actually. Although many people call the trefoil-combination of the Ttiiffsts-dome and the villages of Mikhail and Bakunin "Skyhook City." There are so many people living in this one area, including the small farming collectives strung out along the surface roads leading out of the villages, that we *could* call it a city, I suppose. Ah, here we are."

They walked into a wide circular urban space, well lighted with luminescent globes high overhead on poles around the circumference of the space, with a large Elm tree in the middle spreading its canopy over the entire "square."

"Look! Over there's a table with a trio of Djuiivv sitting alone. Let's join them." William said, hurrying towards them.

Won't it be awkward? I don't speak Galactic; I can't talk to them," Brad said, trotting up beside William.

"No. It's okay. They rarely have anything to say to us, but they like us to talk close around them, for the carbon dioxide. They smell good too. A little like hkkk♎ttt. We're lucky tonight!"

They reached the table and William spit out a string of consonants toward the trio of Djuiivv, who replied with three shrill whistles. He carefully picked each of them up off hir chair and put them on the top of the table. Then he sat down on the far side. The table was low enough that he could see over the scarlet bodies of the Djuiivv. "Sit over there, Brad, so we can talk across them and they can have the benefit of our exhaled cee-oh-two."

Brad noticed that the Djuiivv's (skin?) (*integument?*) was shingled in point-down triangles, each with a moderately sharp point, similar to a pineapple. He could see no eyes, nose, or mouth. *They seem to be mostly mobile plants,* he thought.

He looked around the "square" at the gathering of proles, and noticed a large black-skinned man strolling around and around the tree in a stream of other proles, some of them two-legged but not human, many of the humans in pairs, obviously men and women clutching each other erotically. He could tell the Black was male because, unlike the rest of the crowd, he was completely naked. Brad asked William "Is that naked Black prole the usual sort of thing?" The Djuiivv rustled their tentacles and their integuments as they absorbed the CO_2 he exhaled. Brad put his backpack over his crotch again. *Too many attractive women in public! These people are perverse!"*

"No, that's Naked-John, William replied. "He always says that clothes are unnecessary for humans living on the equator of this planet, where it is always warm. He refuses to use resources unnecessarily." The Djuiivv rustled some more, absorbing CO_2. "And he stays in great shape, as you can see," William continued.

"Yes indeed."

"Because he can't hide anything. And he's so well-endowed –"

"Are we on the equator?" Brad asked, uncomfortable with the topic of another man's genitals, even if he was only a darkie-prole, little better than an animal.

"Yep. Gondwana, this continent, is the only continent on Kayoss. It spreads one hundred-thirty-six degrees longitude along the equator, and an average of fifteen degrees latitude on either side."

"This planet has only the one continent?"

"Well, we have lots of good-sized islands, mostly on or near the equator, except for Trotsky Island, at thirty-six degrees latitude south. A big island, very mountainous. The island has snow more than half the year. Lots of villages to go to for a skiing or tobogganing vacation. Our ancestors settled six kinds of penguins and two kinds of huskies there, and humans who prefer a cooler climate. Kayoss is inclined in its orbit only 13.73 degrees, not 23.45 degrees as is the Earth. There are huge icecaps at both our poles."

William shared wine from the picnic-pack, and before Brad found himself becoming too tipsy, he and William joined the stream of people strolling in a circle around the large center tree. Brad soon became bored with it and they returned to the table. No one was going to discover *him* after years of separation, as William had said sometimes happened to other visitors in Mikhail Village.

After a couple of hours of spraying the Djuiivv with CO_2 while William somewhat drunkenly tried to explain why *no* laws were better than *some,* Brad and William walked slowly and carefully back to their inn. Trudging up the two flights of stairs, they fell nearly senseless into their beds.

The next morning, after a late breakfast of eggs, buttered toast, and bacon which tasted fresh from the pig, although William reminded Brad that all their meat came from vats and no animal had died to feed him, the two men separated for the day, agreeing to meet back at the inn for dinner an hour before sundown. William walked over to Bakunin Village to visit an old friend, and Brad returned to the library and all the information he could get from the library's access to the Kayoss GIL (Global-Information-Link).

To his surprise, he was able to print out maps from the GIL which showed mineral deposits and liquid or gas carboniferous resources, as well as the locations of villages around the globe and what manufacturing or service collectives were headquartered where. He discovered there was an island, Adam-and-Eve Island, where no aliens were welcome, and the humans all lived in a dome which was sealed to prevent aliens from entering, and all around the dome were the fields which fed the humans and provided pasturage for their large meat-animals: goats, pigs, and llamas. They used no vats. They were a splinter-civilization set apart from the alien-loving, vat-meat-eating, Anarkhist-proles Brad was visiting. They had an elected law-making body, an internal money-economy, an everywhere-government, and a quasi-barter economic arrangement with the rest of the humans on Kayoss. Brad decided that Adam-and-Eve Island was where he would locate his seat of government, when he was Viceroy. They were the sorts of proles who would be best suited to serving a Ruler.

He learned that the Anarkhist-proles had several universities, and that each had a variety of courses available, from decorative mat-weaving and botany to advanced astrophysics and cosmology. He also discovered many apprenticeship programs from cooking to agronomics to spatial engineering. *These _Anarkhist_-proles have built quite an interesting society here without the Families to guide them,* Brad thought. *I suppose the aliens have buffered reality for them. Really, that's the only possible explanation for their survival. Otherwise, without the essential dynamics of Capitalism to prop them up, this silly Anarkhist culture would have collapsed long ago.*

Men must be _men_! Free of the weakening influence of

women, they must <u>compete</u> in the struggle for existence, or they degenerate into cute, useless bunny rabbits! While William, he thought, was an agreeable companion, Brad longed for the company of those who understood the reality of existence, of Competition for the Right to Survive, cousins of his Family, with whom he could be honest about his feelings and his dreams.

As he left the library, a sign over the outside door said:

RECYCLE PAPER!
THE TREES WILL THANK YOU FOR IT!

*　　*　　*

William Johnbrown returned to his alma mater, Bakunin Humanities University, to look up his favorite Professor, Davida Louisemichel, who had come to occupy the Red-Emma Chair of Anarkhist Philosophy in the College of Social Studies. She was available most afternoons, as she had told William when he had called from Chomsky Station and made an appointment.

Once settled in the Professor's cool, book-lined study in a comfortable stuffed chair, with a glass of tea near at hand, William told his old Professor about Brad Darsen, and his remark about *"our* proles."

"He seems to be enjoying us, some of the time," William continued. "But I'm afraid he's also thinking how rich we are, and how many resources the Families could exploit."

"How did he get through the Barrier?" Davida asked.

"He didn't say, and I don't think he knows. He was unconscious for nearly the first half of the trip to Alpha

Centauri. I think whoever sent him didn't want to give us any information so we could patch up the Barrier."

"Has anyone up-orbit been investigating his ship?"

"Sure. It has a typical copy of the primitive Q-V drive the Geejjikk invented long ago and spread around the galaxy."

'And nothing in the way of a clever invention that could pierce the Barrier?" Davida asked.

"No," William said sadly. "Just the Q-V drive and lots of robots who ignored us."

"So. We're soon going to be overrun with the Bourgeoisie?"

"That's what I'm afraid of."

"Does he speak often of his home?" the Professor asked.

"Only to talk about their robots and his contempt for women, whom he considers to be animals for sex and breeding only. Nothing about his family or friends. Oh, and people with really dark skin make him uncomfortable."

"Racist, as well as sexist and classist. Hmm?"

"Yes," William said. "Homophobic too, I should guess, as well as anti-Semitic,"

"All those xenophobias seem to go together. You did say he seems to be fascinated with the Djuiivv, though. So we can have some hope he'll become an alien-lover."

"I think the greatest compliment he could pay any of our non-human friends would be to consider them potential business rivals, or partners," William said.

"Well, we know Capitalism inevitably becomes Imperialism, and —" the Professor said.

"That means a willingness to use terrible violence

against those who hold the resources the Capitalists want to exploit," William finished for her.

"Unfortunately correct," she said.

"What can we do to protect ourselves? To protect our whole Galaxy from these rapacious, violent humans?" William asked bleakly.

"We'll need to consult with some of our alien friends, and think this problem through with them. Our own human Kayoss Defense Syndic has already called a conference here at Bakunin University for early next year. They became instantly concerned as soon as Darsen showed up with his pseudo-aristocratic attitude. Of course, scholars all over Kayoss holding a Red Emma Chair, a Sasha Berkman Chair, or a Nestor Makhno Chair of Anarkhist Philosophy were invited to the conference right away. This is a problem all our Galactic species need to solve together. Your bourgeoisie has a long trip home and back with that primitive Q-V drive. Since we have FTL-ships, and the boogees do not, we have time. Almost nine earth-years."

"Thanks, Davida. I knew you could help. And he's not *my B*ourgeoisie."

"Of course not. How about an early supper in my dorm? We've got a great new cook."

"Oh, rats, I can't. I have to meet Brad at our inn for supper an hour before sunset. I've got just enough time to walk. Thanks for the tea. And let me use your toilet before I leave."

"Come and see me again before you go back to Chomsky Station. Okay?" Davida asked William as soon as he came out of the toilet.

'Thanks. I will. And add me to your list for that conference. Okay?"

"Yes indeed."

The two humans hugged warmly and William set off across the campus to the foot-trail which led to Mikhail Village. He walked fast enough to make a slight detour through a public garden he had always enjoyed. The flowers were exquisite as usual.

Brad was quiet at dinner. Apologizing that he must be poor company, he went up alone to their room to pour over the GIL printouts he had made at the library. He fell asleep re-reading the material about Adam-and-Eve Island.

William went out alone. He stopped at a shop and obtained a common wooden flute. It was a new hobby for him, and he wasn't very talented, but he knew that practice wouldn't hurt. There had been no human musicians in the village 'square' the night before. He hoped to find the Djuiivv again and jam with them.

*   *   *

The next morning, William persuaded Brad to join him for a Happening in the dome of the Ttiiffsts.

"Is that the big yellow glass wall we can see out our room's window?" Brad asked.

"Yes, a geodesic dome two and a half miles high, five miles in diameter, full of chlorine and the Ttiiffsts who breathe it. We humans often visit, wearing atmosphere suits of course. We can't understand what the Ttiiffsts are doing in their various Happenings, but we enjoy their aerial ballets. Their iridescent wings are beautiful. I'm glad I found out about this one today. It was posted on the Inter-Species Schedule in our lobby."

It was a short walk to the little blockhouse which served as an airlock for the Ttiiffsts' dome. They struggled into silvery one-piece suits with attached soft zip-up-the-side transparent headpieces. They donned tanks of air like backpacks. William helped Brad and then asked him for help when Brad failed to automatically reciprocate. They were both checked for atmospheric integrity by the Safety-Attendant. Then they entered an airlock, waited while the atmospheres were exchanged, and stepped into the chlorine-filled dome.

It was hard to see things clearly through the yellowness of the Ttiiffsts' atmosphere. But Brad felt comfortable inside his airtight suit, breathing his oxygen-rich air. There were large cone-like structures in view on either side of them. They came to a moving walkway, and William told Brad, "Step on it against the direction of the slideway."

That was easy enough. Brad got on, turned around and stood enjoying the alien scenery they were being carried past. He was no botanist, so the big feathery tree-like plants overhanging the slideway looked okay to him, although they were an odd amber color. The slideway moved them more quickly than a man could trot. Brad looked up, but the roof of the dome was too far overhead for human eyes to see through the yellow, chlorine-air.

Suddenly, there was an irritating, repetitive honk of sound alternating with a loud announcement in the consonant-rich, whistle-filled panGalactic language, and flashing red lights along the edges of the slideway ahead.

Pushing his flexible plastic faceplate against Brad's, William shouted, "There's a big plant fallen down across the slideway ahead!" Grasping the Earthman's upper arm firmly, William pushed him towards the edge of the moving walkway. "Stop here and step off," William said loudly. Several human and alien shapes in silver suits were rushing past them to hurry off.

Confused, when William let go of his arm, Brad tripped over his own feet and fell backward onto the slideway, which – just before it jerked to a stop – moved him quickly into the downed plant. He felt a piercing pain in the side of his right thigh and smelled a sharp trace of chlorine as a broken "branch" tore a hole in his atmosphere-suit. William and several large, brown, fuzzy insects with huge wings quickly descended upon him. He heard William shouting, "Brad! Brad," and several phrases in Galactic. Brad began choking on the chlorine fumes invading his suit. He was terrified, panicked, surrounded by huge creepy insects, and convulsively fighting for air. William held his leg still while one of the insects spun a band around Brad's injured thigh, with silk thread pulled out of its abdominal spinneret by several thin, jointed, clicking legs of waxed chitin. Brad tried, in vain, to pull away from the touch of those stick-like legs.

One of the aliens leaned close to his face, as if peering at him. It ran lacy antenna over the transparent plastic of his faceplate. Brad fought the nausea which burst through his terror. He knew vomiting inside his helmet would be disastrous. Under the antenna, the face of the alien was shinny and hard, with huge faceted compound-eyes, little wiggling "leg"-like things for mouthparts, and short, sharp mandibles. Another of the huge insects extruded some goo from its mouth — It looked to Brad as if the insect were about to bite him! — and using its jointed mouth-"legs," smeared the goo over the silk-covered puncture in his atmosphere suit.

Several of the insects then picked him up and carried him through the yellow air toward the airlock, while William ran alongside shouting, "Brad! You're gonna be all right! We gotcha! We gotcha!"

After the insects set him down, Brad — fighting for air, his nose and throat swollen — lost consciousness while William was dragging him by his shoulders into the airlock.

*   *   *

The Earthman awoke propped-up in a well-made bed with the sheets pulled tight into hospital corners. The antiseptic aroma in the air was oddly familiar. With some difficulty — because they seemed to be glued shut — he opened his eyes, and looked at the room he was in. It contained six beds, five of them empty. The walls were painted off-white. He seemed to be the only patient. Down past his feet, there was an open door to a hallway on the right. His nose and throat burned with pain. There was some plastic thing wrapped around his right thigh where the wound was. The injured leg didn't hurt. There was a long thin plastic tube in his right arm connected to a plastic bag of clear beige liquid hanging from a metal tree beside his head. "Hello?" he called-out in a harsh whisper, futilely hoping to catch the attention of someone who could tell him how he was.

Despite his pain, he was unable to stay awake. When he awoke again, someone was touching him. He cranked open his gummy eyes and saw a pale-skinned young man wearing a spotless white lab coat, holding his wrist, and intently looking at a watch on his own wrist. "Hello?" Brad croaked. His throat was terribly sore. He noticed for the first time that there was a tube in his nose.

"Hello," the young man said, smiling. "So you're with us at last." He looked back at the watch on his wrist.

"How – uhkk – how am I? Where's William?"

"You're going to be fine. I'm your doctor, Mariam Luxemburg, and uh, your friend William has been in several times to bother us, so he'll probably be in soon to see you. Are you hungry?"

Brad considered her words. "Yes, I'm hungry. Very hungry," he snapped impatiently. "Could I have a full breakfast?"

"Certainly, if you think you can eat it. Someone will be by soon with a tray," the strange doctor said.

"Hey, Brad!" William came bustling in the door, a wooden flute in one hand. He had changed his T-shirt for another of the same color but with a different design. "I see the doc has taken good care of you. Hi, Mare," he nodded at the doctor. "How you feeling?" he asked Brad.

"I'll let you know after I get to eat breakfast," Brad replied with worried dignity. He was uncomfortable with the thought that his doctor was a *woman*. And a *Jew*. He had been taught, at an early age, in the Family-schools, that Jews had been a people so sneaky they often appeared to be White, even though they were actually far from it. They had been a whole people who had rejected Jesus – thereby delaying the righteous theocracy he had been bringing to Mankind – and they had been completely eliminated – or so the Families had thought – during the U.S. reign of the Reverend Cletus A. Johnson in the last of the twenty-first century, before the Families had taken direct control to protect their own economic interests. The Reverend Johnson had been the last prole religious leader to have any influence on the worldwide culture of free enterprise which had brought the Families to their unquestioned position of dominance.

A prole pushing a metal cart with food trays stopped out in the hall by the door of Brad's room, and the doctor fetched him a tray, putting it down on a table she swung over his lap. Another prole came into the room pushing a cart with a trio of Djuiivv on it. The three Djuiivv whistled shrilly and one of them spoke the harsh consonants of panGalactic. Brad wondered where the speaking-apparatus was on their vegetable-like bodies.

Following the Djuiivvs in a baggy silver atmosphere suit was a Ttiiffsts, one of the giant insects who breathed chlorine gas. Zee spoke panGalactic by balancing on its middle two limbs and rubbing its back-legs together inside the suit. Brad was shocked to see a nasty-looking stinger attached to the back end of the Ttiiffsts' abdomen. He stopped with a forkful of scrambled eggs halfway to his mouth. Then shrugging – since he hadn't been stung when he was in the chlorine dome close to the Ttiiffsts – he completed the gesture, chewed, and swallowed with some difficulty because his throat was still very sore. He kept his eyes on the giant insect.

William spoke panGalactic to the aliens, then turned to Brad and explained, "The Djuiivv triad here were our companions at the Mikhail Village-Square Party. And this Ttiiffsts is one of the folks who rescued you in their dome. I told them 'thank you,' on your behalf. The Ttiiffsts saved your life, you know. You can smile. They know what we mean by it."

Brad picked up a strip of bacon, and wiggled it at the doctor. He knew *Jews* were frightened of pork products. "What?" he asked William.

"I mean," William explained, "that they know many humans are partially carnivores, but that showing our teeth is not a threat."

"Oh." Brad smiled vaguely, feeling out of sorts. He then thoughtfully ate his bacon, forcing the crispy stuff down his sore throat.

The three Djuiivv spoke some more galactic, one of them holding up with hir tentacles what was obviously a single purplish square of hkkk♎ttt. William said, "Brad, you're in luck. The Djuiivv have brought you some hkkk♎ttt for a get-well present! They know how much we humans like it."

Brad grinned enthusiastically. He saw the three Djuiivv as very cute, and not at all threatening, unlike the insectile Ttiiffsts. "How do I say 'thank you' in Galactic?" he slurped. His mouth was full of saliva, in anticipation of the hkkk⚊ttt. At that moment, he could concentrate on nothing else.

"*Khkkkkttt'hee*" the doctor said, smiling at him.

"*Huwukk-teh-hee*" Brad said with a terrible accent, hampered by his uncooperative throat lining. The three Djuiivv whistled brightly in return.

"Oh," William said, "we have some music to play for your repast. I've been practicing my flute with the Djuiivv." He held up the wooden flute.

The Djuiivv began whistling a very strange sequence of notes, and William joined in with a somewhat human-sounding melody on his flute. The doctor clapped her hands together and beamed at them. In that moment, to Brad's eyes, she looked rather caring, like a good fem, like the old woman — who had seemed almost like a person — who had been their housekeeper when he was a boy.

Brad used his toast and scrambled eggs, and what was left of the bacon, along with some of the hkkk⚊ttt, to make a sandwich. He ate slowly – despite the chlorine damage to his tongue and nose – sipping his breakfast fruit juice often, to moisten his sore throat, savoring the wonderful alien-flavor of the hkkk⚊ttt combined with the common tastes of earth-food. He listened to the amazingly sweet sounds of the Djuiivv and William "whistling" together. Other proles crowded into the doorway to listen.

*   *   *

Brad spent several more days in bed. The wound in his leg was healing slowly. His *doctor!* had explained to him he must not move that leg for a few days. It was necessary to expose the open wound to a nearly 100% oxygen-and-medicine mist in the short plastic tunnel his thigh rested in during the healing process. And he was given frequent breathing therapy, a soothing mist given with a mask over his nose and mouth. He was told the damage to his respiratory system from the chlorine-air was worse than the wound in his leg. After the first morning when he woke up, he was given bland, warm, creamed, fruit-laced cereal for breakfast every day, since his doctor believed he could not possibly enjoy bacon and eggs. Brad missed the eggs, and even the bacon, despite his continuing sore throat, and despite his medical problems, he felt injured in his massive, fragile Family-ego and sense of entitlement.

Brad's doctor, Mariam Luxemburg, was so knowledgeable and competent, and had such a good bedside manner, he often forgot she was a woman. Her short curly auburn hair, and the loose labcoat she always wore, hiding whatever breast development she might have had, completed the illusion of maleness. She told him that, although of course some people were, she wasn't Jewish. Luxemburg was the name of the village where she had been born and raised, named after Rosa Luxemburg, an important historical figure as far as the proles were concerned. Brad reflected that it was lucky she wasn't a **dark**-prole, or he would have been totally unable to conveniently forget, for long stretches of time, that she wasn't a *Man* of the Families.

William visited daily, although there was never a repeat of the impromptu concert Brad had been given on first awakening. One afternoon, with bright summer sunlight filling the room, the two men sat talking about the – to Brad – *strange* Anarkhist customs of Kayoss, when Brad's doctor came in and announced that Brad should get up and exercise his leg.

"Now?" Brad asked anxiously. "You still have that plastic baggie on my thigh. I don't think the muscle is strong enough yet."

"Lying around not using your muscles is bad for them, Brad," the doctor said. "Come on up. We'll help. Will, take his left side."

The three of them staggered slowly around the room – William and the doctor mostly holding him up – as Brad winced each time his right leg took his weight.

"Okay. That's enough," the doctor said. "We'll sit you down. Now lie down. Okay. We'll put the 'baggie' back on, to protect the wound." She put the plastic sheath on over his right foot and carefully pulled it up to cover the open wound on his thigh. Then she adjusted the breathing mask over his face and turned on the healing mist for him to inhale. "You can rest now," she said, smiling, sitting down on the bed beside him and taking his hand in a warm comforting grip.

"Uh, Brad, I'll be back to see you tomorrow," William said, walking quickly to the door.

"No! Wait! Bill!" Brad hooted through the plastic over his mouth and nose.

William paused and leaned smiling against the doorjamb. "I can see your doctor needs to talk to you about a few things." Then he turned and left.

"Uh….." Brad looked at his doctor, and did not know what to say. She was still holding one of his hands.

"William tells me our society here on Kayoss makes you uncomfortable," she said.

"No … not … uncomfortable," he said. "Just … well … all of you are very different from what I was taught about basic human nature."

"I understand you don't think women are human beings. That we are not people."

"No. uh … actually, you are very different from any woman I have ever known."

"I see … So, what are the women like, whom you have known?"

"Quiet, submissive, uh … focused on sex and uh, having babies."

"Just what men want them to be, and no more. Right?"

"Right. Well, that *is* God's plan for women, isn't it? Aren't you all well-built for having babies?"

"Women also have a brain as large as men's."

"No. No, not really. That isn't true," he said, vigorously shaking his head.

"Oh? I suppose you have performed as many autopsies as I have. Or you have personally weighed and measured thousands of the brains of men and women. And have statistical proof of your beliefs?"

"Well, no, but I have read the writings of many medical men who had practiced medicine long enough in the nineteenth, twentieth, and twenty-first centuries to have observed that women are ruled by their hormones, and are clearly incapable of intellectual thought."

"But you don't think that testosterone – in which all men are awash all the time – interferes with intellectual thought. Right?" She was still holding his hand.

Brad pulled his hand free. "Well, the strength of testosterone, which we recognize, is the reason all men of the Families are encouraged to buy a wife at the beginning of their adult lives, so they can have sexual release whenever they need it, so sexual need will not interfere with business or the important work of a man."

"So," she said quietly, sadly, "Sex for you is for release only, not for communication, pleasure, and sharing with another human being. Not for love. I'm so sorry."

"Sorry! You don't need to feel sorry for me!" His sore leg and sore throat made him irritable. "I'm a member of the United Families of Earth! We are the best part of the human race! *We* don't need the help of aliens to have a civilization! Ahrrrrrrrrr!" he growled, and turned away, showing her his back.

Dr. Mariam Luxemburg reluctantly left the room. *Brad was her patient first of all*, and he would heal better without the aggravation of having his sexist world-view severely challenged.

At the coordinating-niche at the end of the hall, near the elevator, William Johnbrown was leaning against the high desk and talking intently with a young dark-skinned man with several short dredlocks crowning the top of his head like a little hat. He wore the blue cotton pants and starched white scrub of an apprentice healthcare-Worker.

William turned to the doctor, "So, Mare, how's it going with Brad?"

"Worst case of testosterone poisoning I've ever seen, Will. He thinks women are fuck-holes and baby-machines, not people. Pisses me off."

"I see some interest there, in him, for you."

"I wish I didn't find him so attractive. . . ."

"There's reason for hope. I think."

"I'll be glad to see him released," she snapped.

"I'll talk to him…" William said.

"No! Don't you *dare!*" She turned to the apprentice: "Greg, hook Darsen's leg wound, in eleven-A, up to a mist of O_2 and 30% gelkazine, would you? It's time. Oh, and check he has enough nanobots in his breatholyzer jar."

"Sure, Doc," the apprentice said. Will," he said, slapping William affectionately on the shoulder. "See you next Thursday at the Purple Street Kemmerhouse." He walked off quickly to his work.

"You've always been one for sexual adventure, Mare," William said quietly.

"I don't know, Will," she whispered, shaking her head.

"I think you, of anyone, can change his mind about women."

"A challenge, huh?"

"No, just a cross-cultural sharing, I think."

"And Andy?"

"You know she doesn't care what you do while she's away on Chomsky Station. Just don't get pregnant, please."

"You know we have our family planned. I won't mess that up. And Brad would be possessive, wouldn't he?"

"Especially if it was a boy, I would suppose."

"Yes."

"So?" he asked, raising one eyebrow.

"Oh, I guess I'll give him a try, if I can," she said. "Maybe I can help him escape from his bigoted, Imperialistic worldview, which is clearly making him unhappy. I better requisition an anti-fertility patch."

The healing-facility provided Brad with a com-pad and access to the GIL, and he was able to continue his researches into the underground metallic and carbonaceous resources of the planet Kayoss. William stopped by daily to see him and provide him with the friendly masculine company he craved. He was not bored the few days he was mostly confined to his bed. But he found he was always happiest each day when Dr. Luxemburg came in to check on him. Just seeing her come through the door of his room made him feel warm all over. Despite himself – and while he continued to try and remember that his doctor was a *woman* and therefore not a person – Brad grew to like her very much.

With daily exercise of his wounded leg, he was soon able to get up and walk around by himself, using only a cane for stability. Without admitting to himself what he was doing, he began to watch Dr. Luxemburg as she worked. She was apparently the only full-fledged, non-apprentice doctor on staff. There were few inpatients in the West-Mikhail Healing Clinic and Trauma Center, the facility where he was recuperating.

Besides caring for the out-patients who came in, Dr. Luxemburg also saw each inpatient every day. And the first time he realized she was just as warm and concerned with all the other patients as she was with him, Brad could not understand why he was upset. When she came into his room to see him that day, he was stiff and cold with her, quickly snapping his answers to her quiet questions about his breathing.

"Brad, are you having some pain in your leg? Maybe you're not healing as well as we thought." She lifted the gauze bandage over the wound on his right thigh.

He pushed her hands away. "I'm all right. Leave me alone." He rubbed his hands over his upper thighs. He stared at his left foot. He couldn't look at her. There was a strange tightness in his chest that had nothing to do with the chlorine damage.

"Brad, what's the matter?

"Nothing." He still couldn't look at her.

"Do you need me to get you another doctor, a male?"

"No!" He looked at her quickly, and then turned his head away again.

The doctor reminded herself it was her friend Will Johnbrown's opinion that Brad Darsen was as attracted to her as she was to him. "You know, Brad," she said. "I was hoping to get to know you better once you are no longer my patient. William told me I could take over showing you around our society, if you like."

"You would? You're not just being nice because I'm your patient?"

"No." She was puzzled.

"You're nice to all your patients." It was an accusation.

"I like my work, Brad. And a pleasant atmosphere is essential to healing any patient. But sometimes a doctor begins to like certain patients beyond the need to provide a healing atmosphere, as in your case." She picked up his hand again, and held it tenderly.

"You like me?" he asked. "You want to get to know me better?"

"Yes."

"Oh. Uh … I find it very strange to meet a woman who makes her own choices. And wants to choose *me*."

"Maybe you'll even be able some day to see me as a real **person**," she said, grinning wryly at him.

Just then an alarm began pulsing through the hall. A human in blue pants and white scrub popped (his?)(her?) head in the door of Brad's room. "Doctor? It's Anna Trotsky, in nine-B. Come quick."

Doctor Luxemburg dropped Brad's hand without hesitation, and left the room in a rush, without a backward glance.

Brad waited the rest of the afternoon for her to return. He was not used to wanting a woman who had her own professional responsibilities to fulfill, rather than always waiting patiently upon *his* needs and pleasure, as he was used to from his wife as well as the one hooker whose body, time, and skills he had once purchased.

Dr. Luxemburg stopped by to see him in the early evening. The light in the room was dim. Brad tried to hide his feelings of irritation and impatience. Having to stop himself from snapping at a woman because she was not perfectly attendant upon him was a new experience for Brad, but he sensed he had a better chance of sexing her if he treated her like a person, however strange the entire concept was to him. As a man who owned a wife, Brad was used to regular sex, of which he'd had *none* since his father – *damn him!* – had put him aboard a starship and blasted him off to Alpha Centauri.

"Brad," Dr. Luxemburg said hurriedly, "I'm going off duty now for a couple of weeks." She sat down on the edge of his bed, as she had done several times before, and held his hand again in both of hers.

Brad's chest tingled with delight, a confusing feeling for him. His breathing quickened.

"I've left orders for the relief-doc to let you out of here tomorrow after breakfast," she continued, "if you're still in as good shape as you seem to be right now. You'll be provided with directions and materials so you can finish taking care of your leg yourself, and keep up with your breathing treatments. . ."

"Okay," he gasped. He was, at that very moment, having trouble with his breathing, even though his throat did not hurt as much as it had before.

"Brad, I live near the clinic. I'd like you to come and see me tomorrow when you get out of here. It's number thirteen in the Court of the Red Virgin off Rainbow Avenue. Here's a map."

All right! Brad thought triumphantly to himself. "Okay, sure, Doctor," he said, fighting the grin that twitched on his face.

"Mariam, please. See you tomorrow."

LOVE IN ANARKHY

William came to see Brad right after breakfast the next morning, and after the relief-doctor had discharged him, William offered to take the healing materials Brad was given for self-care to their room in the inn. Brad thanked him, and set out – with his pack on his back – to find Rainbow Avenue and The Court of the Red Virgin. He asked directions on the street several times, picking the most pale-skinned proles to talk to. He walked slowly with his cane, favoring his injured right leg. At one point, along Rainbow Avenue, around a bend, on one side of the street, a field of (*wheat*?) stretched almost to the horizon. Shortly, on the other side of the street, he found a sign with an arrow pointing into the Court of the Red Virgin.

The courtyard was floored with bluish slate between varnished wooden containers planted with bright flowers. Turning in a semicircle, Brad found one of the skinny four-story buildings was marked "13." Inside the outer front door, there was an alcove with two call buttons marked "Jaxson-&-Alicia" and "Andrea-&-Mariam." He rang the button with Mariam's name, wondering if her roommate was home. *Can't a <u>doctor</u> afford to live alone?* he thought.

"Who is it?" the grill below the button crackled.

"Uh, Brad Darsen."

"Come on in! The door is unlocked."

Brad stepped into the inner hall. A wooden stairway curved up on his right and a door on his left opened to reveal a smiling young woman in beige shorts and a red t-shirt. "Brad! I'm glad you could make it," she said.

"Hello, uh, Mariam," Brad said, noticing she had *noticeable breasts* under her t-shirt. He held his backpack in front of his crotch to hide his rising erection.

She made him comfortable with coffee at a table in her large sunny kitchen, overlooking a backyard filled with greenery. Apprehensive, not knowing how to act, he gripped his coffee cup hard enough to snap the handle. In the confusion of his apologies and her mopping up the hot coffee, they found themselves in a standing embrace and he discovered she was slightly taller than he was. Still clutching each other, they moved to a small room off the hall, hastily undressed, and tumbled onto a soft bed covered with a crisp cotton sheet.

Once lying down naked together, the difference in their heights was not apparent. She wound her long legs around him and suddenly he was inside her and they were moving together without his having to worry – as he often had with his wife – that he was not hard enough yet.

The physical sensation was the same, but it was all somehow *different.* Not just his penis, but his whole body was on fire. He was consumed with joy. Whenever he found himself on top, he looked down at her face and saw a person . . . *a person!* . . . overcome with pleasure, her eyes as warm and caring as when she had been only his doctor. She was uninhibited and free and made as much noise as the hooker – never his wife! – had made when she was faking pleasure. But Mariam's response was real and wonderfully eager.

This time Brad wasn't *alone* in the grip of desire, as he always felt he had been during every sexual experience of his life thus far, either masturbating or with a woman. *Mariam* was with him, just as hungry, just as joyful, just as pleasured by the simple act of coitus as he was. When she genuinely exploded with orgasm, he followed her with his own, crying with ecstasy, overwhelmed by the *shared* experience**. *For the first time in his life!***

He fell asleep. She woke him up when she brought in a bedside tray of coffee, milk and cookies. "Try to keep crumbs off the sheet," she said. "I hope to be using it again soon,"

"With me?"

"Yes." She smiled at him.

He felt his heart melt and gum up his lungs so he was breathless again for a moment. "Then it is to my advantage to be careful with crumbs," he gasped.

She was sitting like a man on the edge of the bed, her right ankle balanced on her left knee. But she was not a man. Brad resolutely put aside his confusion and decided to enjoy whatever he could in the strange situation.

After more sex – slower, less rushed, more whole-body sensual, and more delicious than the first – Mariam sent him off to his room at the inn near the Skyhook with a promise to come by the next day to get him for lunch.

"Bill! Bill! Why didn't you tell me how great sex is with a free female?" Brad gushed as soon as he entered their room on the third floor of the inn. He was huffing, out of breath after hobbling up two flights of stairs. His chest hurt.

"Brad, sit down. Come on now. How could I tell you?"

"Why not?"

"Well ... you have to experience things like that for yourself, don't you?"

"Oh, I guess."

"You wouldn't have believed me, anyway."

*   *   *

Mariam arrived, as promised, late the next morning, wearing a wicker-basket as a backpack filled with picnic-fixings. They went out together to catch an electric "train" without tracks to the Village of Bakunin.

At the train-stop in Mikhail Village where they waited, there were two trios of Djuiivv also waiting for the train. When it arrived, Marian and the driver of the train picked up each of the Djuiivv and set them in a small roofed car, (standing?)(sitting?) on the seats. At her suggestion, Brad helped. He found the Djuiivv had several short tentacles on their flat bottoms which enabled them to walk about slowly. Mariam explained to Brad, once they were seated facing the six aliens, that the Djuiivv often counted on humans or other oxygen-breathing aliens to pick them up and move them about, since they were so small and slow compared to the humans and other aliens living on Kayoss.

"You mean those Djuiivv and the other aliens are *residents* of Kayoss, not just visitors?" Brad asked, shocked.

"Certainly. In the civilized galaxy, all planets are inhabited by more than one species, so we can all enjoy sharing the world-view of other aliens."

"You mean, humans can never have a planet of their own?"

"Well, Kayoss is a planet mostly of humans, named by humans, organized by humans, with a predominately human culture. Aliens like the Djuiivv are a minor, but important, part."

"I'm not sure I like that," he mumbled.

"Oh, but we want to enjoy the presence of other sapient species. It's one of the great things about being a member of a galaxy-wide culture. You like the Djuiivv, don't you?"

"Yes." But I've seen so many other creatures. . . . Don't you have enough variety with so many different human races living here?"

"There is only <u>one</u> human race, Brad."

"What? What about the darkies?"

"Oh! You mean people with different amounts of melanin in their skin? Well, we're all mongrels, all we *'proles,'* as I guess you think of us. We're all descended from every shade of the former working-class peoples of Earth, from all over the globe, and, on Kayoss, the mixing was recent enough that wide differences in skin colour pop up all the time. Other species have differences in colour too. The Geejjikk are all different shades of green, for instance."

"Takes some getting used to," he mumbled.

"That's okay," she said, you'll get there." She threw her arm around Brad as they sat together facing six enigmatic Djuiivv on an electric train winding its way through the clean uncluttered streets of Mikhail Village. She whistled at the Djuiivv and they whistled back, rustling happily in response to the extra CO_2 in the air.

At one point the train took a suspension-bridge over a mile-wide field of corn, to city streets on the other side, and thus to the Bakunin Village Green, which was scattered with picnic tables and divided into some semi-private sections by thick rows of berry bushes. Brad remembered to help lay out the picnic things after Mariam put down a blanket on the grass. Then, as they were propped up on their elbows sharing the food Marian had packed, he asked her why there was a field of corn, and a field of wheat, as he had seen the day before, inside the Village limits.

"It's an old idea," she said, "from some radical architects on Earth a few centuries ago — Christopher Alexander and his colleagues — based on the understanding that human beings need contact with nature and green growing things, and that *'when the countryside is far away, the city becomes a prison.'* Our villages are designed so that 'fingers' of countryside about one mile wide stretch into the village, and 'fingers' of the village less than one mile wide stretch out into the countryside, always with public transportation. So we live next to the land which grows our food, never forgetting the natural environment we need as the natural animals we are."

"It's very strange….." he said.

"You have separate domes, on Earth, don't you, for edible crops?" she asked.

"Yes, and the crops are tended by robots. . . ."

"And the – proletariat? – is that the full word?" she asked.

"Yes, the proles."

"So," she said, "the humans, the proles — who are not members of the ruling Families — live outside the Domes in the pollution created by four hundred years of dirty manufacturing, lumber-milling, and mining?"

"Sure. The proles aren't much use to us, except for the ones who get a good technical education, and the polluted lands aren't much use either – they've been strip-mined or otherwise used up, or are covered with city-slums – so we of the Families don't pay much attention to the few dirty proles who are left from years ago, except for those we allow to live in the Domes, whom we need to work to program or repair our bots."

"My ancestors were those proles from Earth who were lucky enough to be rescued by the Geejjikks and their great ships," she said quietly.

He thought fast. "And I am glad they were," he said, raising his glass to her in a silent toast, and smiling what he hoped she would see as a fond, sexy smile. *Rescued by squishy green aliens!* he thought to himself, hiding from her a jolt of contempt that felt like a knife in his chest.

He and Mariam toured museums and various semi-automated factories during the day, and concerts or village festivals in the evenings. He rarely saw William in the room they supposedly shared at the inn because Brad often spent the night with Mariam and had breakfast with her before they went out each day to explore "Skyhook City." Daily, she re-dressed and re-medicated the wound on his leg and made him sit still for his breathing treatments. He began to suspect that perhaps the Families were wrong to reject the pleasure of living with women. The joy of waking up happy every day in bed next to a woman he cared about was something he had never suspected could be possible.

One day after breakfast, Mariam took him to a factory not far from her domicile. The factory used nanobots to grow sunscreens of thin-layer-silica photovoltaic cells to be used for solar power. The proles who worked there — mostly people from her neighborhood, Mariam told him — served as programmers for the nanobots, and as inspectors at various levels of the work. They were a cheerful bunch, obviously enjoying each other's company, occasionally laughing spontaneously at each other's jokes. Brad was surprised to see proles so obviously enjoying their work. He said so to Mariam.

"You find it strange that people could enjoy working?" she asked.

"Yes, because proles, we know from history, have had to be *forced* to produce things. We have always known that if they didn't need money to survive, the lazy proles would not work at all."

"This is one of those times when yours and my world-views are in serious conflict," Mariam said.

"Why are these proles here?" he asked. "Much of the work appears to be repetitive. Why don't you have robots doing it?"

"People enjoy working. And we believe happy, cooperative, self-motivated Workers do better work than robots."

"You *are* using robots here: nanobots."

"In this case, the nanobots are doing a job no human being could do, working at a sub-microscopic, molecular level. But the humans as programmers and inspectors are important, in fact irreplaceable, because they bring creativity and pride of accomplishment to the job, something we couldn't get from robots."

"Proles cost more than robots. That's where the saving is made."

"We don't have a money economy. In fact, we learned long ago that in a cooperative, S*ocialist* society, <u>*Workers are the real wealth.*</u>"

"Socialist? I thought this was an A*narkhist* society."

"Philosophically, Anarchism is an outgrowth of Socialism. We removed the hierarchy and the elitist bureaucracy of those great Socialist experiments which ultimately failed on Earth. From the way our ancestors had survived on earth when the biosphere began to crash and the Families started using robots as Workers, we had reason to believe that a self-organized Anarkhist people, without a central power structure, could provide the human race – that is, ourselves – with freedom as well as economic survival."

"Why would people work without the need for money?"

"Not having anything to do is terribly boring. No one wants to be useless. Everyone wants to feel they are contributing their own unique skills to make life good for themselves, their family, and their neighbors. And there's a real joy in doing something one is good at, using the time of one's life to make one's mark upon our free society, to do a job that needs to be done."

"Does everyone work without coercion? Is there no one on this planet who gets away with doing nothing?"

"If a person tries to get through life without working at all, zee will have no friends, because friends are usually made at work, and family will fall away, embarrassed to be known as related to a parasite. Parasites — as we call those who do not contribute their skills to our civilization — will wind up having to eat alone, cook alone, live alone, sex alone. A life without companionship, without friends who love you and respect you, without social-sex, without family, would be a horrible life, wouldn't you think?"

"I am not working here. Why do you-all tolerate that?"

"You are a visitor now, on vacation. If you stay with us, we will expect you to work."

"What will I be expected to do?"

"Whatever you're good at, whatever interests you."

"I won't have to dig ditches, or shovel horse manure?"

"Not unless you want to rotate through odd jobs, not bother to have a steady career, and work at something different nearly every day."

"Oh."

*   *   *

One evening, they went to a sports stadium in East Mikhail to see a basketball game. The size of the audience seemed strange to Brad, because on Earth professional (paid) sports had long ago ceased to generate profit for anyone, and were therefore obsolete. He had participated in baseball and basketball tournaments on Earth, but not in exhibition to large crowds. Sports were only a pleasant diversion for young men who were still living on their consultant stipends.

The stands were full of people, not all of them human.

Mariam waved at someone in the stands above the aisle where they came in, and she led Brad up to a bench already partly occupied by a tall dark-green amorphous blob she introduced as Geep, a Geejjikk.

A trumpet-shaped extrusion came out the side of the Geejjikk nearest to Brad, and said, "Hello, Earth-human," in English!

Brad tried to be calm and sophisticated, addressing a green blob: "Uh, hello. I didn't know any Galactics could speak English."

"We Geejjikk are so malleable," Geep answered, "we can reproduce any sounds we have ever heard." The Geejjikk inclined hir trumpet upwards, and spat out a peal of music sweet enough and loud enough to announce the coming of angels.

People around them, human and otherwise, threw candy bars and popcorn balls at the Geejjikk who quietly absorbed them into its body, saying softly to Brad, "The power of my voice is rarely appreciated on this planet. I am constantly aggrieved."

Mariam rescued the Earthman from having to continue the strange conversation with Geep by saying, "Brad, we've going to have to look out for these Ttiiffsts. Let me show you how."

Three Ttiiffsts in their baggy silver atmosphere suits were moving into the stands right in front of them. They crouched in a manner which aimed their stingers directly at the person seated behind them. Brad noticed the stinger of the Ttiiffst sitting right in front of him did seem to have a colorless rubber ball blunting its point.

"Take these straps," Mariam said, handing him two thick silvery strips of material which were attached to the atmosphere suit of *'his'* Ttiiffst. "Hold one in each hand, like this." She demonstrated her grip with the straps she held which were attached to *'her'* Ttiiffst.

"Can I ask why?" Brad said.

"The Ttiiffsts are a winged species, but the atmosphere suits can't be constructed to free their wings. In the excitement of watching the game, the Ttiiffsts always forget they can't fly, and they leap up, trying to throw themselves into the air, and if they aren't held back, with those straps I gave you, they would damage their wings trying to snap them open inside their suits. Also, they would fall down these steep stands and kill themselves, and injure many other people in the stands below."

"What if I get excited and forget about holding on to them?"

"Don't worry, you won't be excited at the same time as the Ttiiffsts. We haven't had an accident in this village in several decades."

"I won't be excited at the same time?" he asked.

"No," she said. "The Ttiiffsts enjoy our basketball games for reasons we humans cannot understand –"

"Nor can we Geejjikk," Geep trumpeted softly on Brad's other side.

"They will all stand up together, trying to flap their wings and rub their legs together," she continued. "And they all do this simultaneously, when nothing is going on, as far as the rest of us are concerned. When we humans come to a basketball game, we know there is a good chance we will have to look out for Ttiiffsts. If you don't think you can do it, we can probably find somewhere else to sit."

"No," Brad said. "I can do it. It's okay."

"Good. I would have been embarrassed to move. Thanks, Brad." *Well, William did think he had the makings of an alien-lover*, she thought, smiling at him.

"So, Earthman," the green blob beside Brad said, patting him softly with a dry — not squishy — pseudopod. "We Geejjikk are responsible for you humans being out here in the galaxy with the rest of us, and we have made a study of all your recreational activities. So let me explain about tournament basketball on Kayoss. We Geejjikk are heartbroken it is a game we cannot play, although you'll notice one of us is a referee."

"Okay," Brad said. "Go ahead."

Very soon, the Geejjikk referee on the playing floor far below – who was coloured a very pale green, almost translucent – trumpeted notice of the game beginning. Zee threw up the ball with one pseudopod, two humans jumped after it, and the game began.

The first quarter went very quickly. Brad found he easily understood the game and it was exciting. The players were all young, tall, and human. Not all male, however. He couldn't understand why the females' breasts did not get in their way, or how the men playing with them were not distracted by the luscious, healthy bodies of the women among them.

The Ttiiffsts sat very quietly during the first quarter's play. During the break between quarters – when nothing much was going on, not even an argument between a coach and a referee – suddenly, all the Ttiiffsts in the stadium leaped up and tried to throw themselves into the air, held back by determined humans and other similarly-shaped species. Brad was absurdly proud he was able to fulfill his part of the responsibility. He glanced over at Mariam, who was completely absorbed in holding her Ttiiffst back. Once the Ttiiffsts settled down, Geep patted him again, and quietly trumpeted congratulations.

That night in Mariam's bed, Brad felt like a Greek god. He was brilliant, tireless, and immortal in his erotic power. She was obviously thrilled with him. He did not fall asleep afterward, but instead lay on his back with her head on his shoulder, listening to the soft purr of her snoring, grinning to himself with such delight he was glad his smile of triumph did not crack his face.

*   *   *

Brad thought to himself that he might be able to stay on Kayoss as the Viceroy, with Mariam, and escape his father. *It would be great to be happy for a change.* He vaguely realized he had never been really happy before. He had always been the most minor, the least loved of his father's sons, the least regarded of his cousins. He had been, at best, entertained, diverted from his essential loneliness. *They'll all have respect for me when I'm the rich Viceroy of this planet I've found. I'll have a half- dozen of wives like Mariam, who will all love me, and be proud to be my wives!*

As the weeks went on, Brad was surprised he never

grew tired of sex with Mariam, as he had with his wife at the femhouse after only a few weeks. He continued to yearn for Mariam when they were not in bed together.

He was also surprised that everything around him – the well-built, sparsely-decorated buildings of the villages; the utilitarian inner spaces; the well-tended trees, flowers, vegetables, and food-grains of their outdoor spaces; as well as the proles and the strange aliens he saw everywhere – were magically more attractive to him than before Mariam had come into his life. Everywhere they went was suffused with an inner golden light which had nothing to do with the gold of their tropical sun. He remembered some of the twentieth century movies he had seen, those movies full of women as part of society. Could it be he was experiencing *Romantic Love?* He, a member of the UFE and a published historical scholar of some reputation among his peers?

One morning, they went back to bed after breakfast. During a lull in the love-making, he was idly exploring her body with his hands, until he came to her feet. She had no toes, none at all. "What?" he said. "I thought you were always wearing beige socks. Why don't you have any toes?"

"I have varleypeds."

"What?" He pulled his hands away from her toeless feet.

"Varleypeds. My parents had me altered with gene-surgery when I was a little fetus. So I have all the bones of an ordinary human foot, but the ends of my 'feet' do not separate into toes with toenails. Lots of humans have varleypeds. Our mutual friend, William, does. It's common on Kayoss. We're hoping the genetic alteration will eventually migrate into the reproductive cells, so future kids will be born already with varleypeds, without the need for fetal surgery. It's a dominant change, an intentional mutation, so only one parent will need to pass it on."

"Intentional mutation?"

"Sure, why not change the basic human body, speed up evolution, now we have the scientific skill to do so? For instance, no human being on Kayoss under the age of ninety has an appendix."

"Oh. Who or what is varley?"

"A terrific science fiction writer. from twentieth and twenty-first century Earth. His stuff is still readable today. He first suggested the idea of feet like socks, without separate toes."

"Well, I guess they're not so bad," Brad said.

"Gee, thanks. I'm glad you don't hate my peds."

"How could I? They're part of you, and I can't hate *you*."

"Good, and speaking of my parents, I'm going to go to visit them. They're on Johann-Most Island, still living in Luxemburg Village. Want to come with me? You haven't really experienced the planet Kayoss if you always stay in one 'city,' on our one continent. Kayoss really is the islands."

"Oh, okay. When do we start?"

"There's a boat leaving this afternoon from Bakunin Harbor for a regular trip to Most Island. We can be on it. Do you want to come with me?"

"Uh, sure. Maybe I should go back to the inn and pack."

She pulled him into her arms. "I had other plans for the rest of the morning. You don't need to pack. You have your backpack and toothbrush here already. And you have everything else you need, as far as I'm concerned. . . ."

No woman had ever touched him so wonderfully with her hand without being ordered to do so. He decided he didn't need to pack. . . .

*   *   *

Brad had been unaware how close to the ocean they were in Mikhail Village. "I've never seen an ocean before," he told Mariam. "It's so *big*."

"Why have you never seen an ocean? Doesn't Earth have oceans?"

"Sure, but my Family lives inland, near the ruined city of Cleveland."

"Wasn't Cleveland on the Great Lakes?"

"Well, I was never much of a traveler. Never left the Family Domes. Too expensive to fly, and too expensive in bodyguard fees to travel any other way."

"Bodyguard fees?"

"Sure. The wild lands of the slums between the civilization of the Domes are too dangerous. Except for the few proles the families employ, most of the proles are murderous thieves, who will kill any Family member they see, and steal whatever he has."

"An inevitable result of the *huge* gap between the rich and the Poor," she muttered.

Brad heard her, but he pretended not to, knowing any discussion of the *inevitable* gap between winners and losers would probably damage any chance he had for more great sex with her, and he didn't want that to happen. He was only on Kayoss to survey the resources. He was not required to convince any of the proles they would be better off living in a free Capitalist society when the Darsen Family took over and he was Viceroy.

He would be a good Viceroy, he knew. His financial laws would be fair, and only congenital losers would fail to thrive on *his* planet. He would make a place for the Djuiivv too. They would prosper greatly by providing hkkk♎ttt to him at his palace every day. . . .

"Brad? Brad!"

He tumbled out of his hazy daydream. "Huh?"

"You're going to need a hooded jacket, if we stay on deck for any part of the trip. I brought one for you. Here." Like a valet, she was holding a jacket for him to slip into.

"Thanks, Mariam." He shrugged the jacket up on his shoulders and they joined a line of people going up a gangplank to board the boat. He glanced uneasily over the side of the plank at the water sloshing between the fat round hull of the boat and the dock.

They found a place at the bow, standing close together, arms entwined. The ocean stretched to the horizon, roughened with the white lace of little waves. Once they were out of the encircling arms of Bakunin Harbor, and the land of Gondwana Continent had fallen far behind them, Brad had to fight with himself not to gibber in fear at the ocean's terrible immensity, unmanning himself in front of his woman.

After a while, to Brad's great relief, Mariam suggested they get out of the cold wind. Below decks there was the usual sharing of food by the travelers. Mariam had brought a large container of fruit salad, and was applauded for her contribution. The shared supper was mostly sandwiches again, sliced vat-meat with lettuce, ketchup, and mustard, without hkkk♎ttt because there were no Djuiivv traveling with them. Brad moped with disappointment.

However, rather than be left alone without her, away from the vastness of the ocean, in the crowded safety of the hold, Brad agreed to return to the deck with Mariam after they ate.

The sun, *Che*, dove quickly into the water behind them as they sped east over the ocean. Bakunin Village was at the far eastern edge of Gondwana, the continent. Most Island was almost two longitude degrees east of the continent.

When the sun set, the stars came out. Brad experienced an intense and sudden vertigo. The ocean was calm that night, and all the stars were reflected in the water. Surrounded by the faintly winking stars, the boat and its passengers seemed to be suspended in outer space. Brad clutched the rail in front of him for security. He felt he could spin off the boat and fall forever into that endless field of stars. Mariam put her arms around him from behind, and he rested against her, feeling safer and more himself than he ever had in his life.

"Beautiful, isn't it, Brad?"

"Yes," he whispered.

"I'm hoping you'll like Kayoss enough, you'll want to stay here with us and not go back to Earth."

He turned in her arms and stood on his toes to kiss her

warm mouth. "I'll think about it," he said. "Do you folks have need of an historical anthropologist?"

"Sure. You can probably teach at a University."

"It would have to be a university near you," he said.

"I'd like that," she said. "I'm sure it can be arranged."

The deck of the Glockenspiel — for that was the name of the boat they were on — was carrying sturdy bags of grain under a large tarp, which the passengers made use of to sit upon and lean against, as the evening wore on and the little boat chugged toward Most Island. Mariam was carrying a warm woolen blanket in her backpack. She and Brad wrapped it around themselves, and burrowed deeper into the embrace of the bag of wheat they had claimed as their makeshift bed.

Brad lay next to Mariam, feeling a warm sense of companionship, since the situation was too cold to think about sex. He had never before felt so comfortable, so much at ease, surrounded by proles of different colors, many of them women. He cuddled next to his own woman, free of pain, anxiety, or the existential loneliness he had felt all his life.

He wondered to himself what he was going to do. Would he become the Viceroy – with the help of the Darsen assault-bots – of a radically changed and conquered planet Kayoss, which he would re-name "Darsen?" Or would he stay with Mariam, forget about Earth and his damned uncaring Family, and become a university professor? He thought, with Mariam's help, he might make a good life for himself on Kayoss. He could escape forever the nagging sense of failure he had carried all his life, despite the publishing success of *A Turning Point*. Growing up the youngest of four brothers, with a father who was rigidly authoritarian, he had accepted the role of the quiet, useless, incompetent baby brother. He had had no choice.

Feeling sleepily confused and yet unworried – for he did not have to make a decision right then – Brad drifted off to sleep on the strange boat, beside the strange woman who had become so important to him, feeling comfortable among all the multi-colored proles around them, warm and safe amid the strange cold stars filling the big ocean sky and reflected in the water, seemingly under the boat as well as overhead.

In the morning, Brad went to the stern of the boat and relieved his bladder over the rear gunwale, standing along with several others. He noticed – yep: breasts, no penis – some of those producing an arching stream of urine were women. *Women who can pee standing up!* he thought, shocked and disgusted. *Is there nothing these Kayoss women will not steal from men?* He was glad Mariam was not among them. The male proles paid no attention to the women urinating alongside them.

Breakfast was a bowl of granola mixed with a cup of plain yogurt and topped by whatever fruits were left from Mariam's offering of the night before. Several people who had spent the night in the hold had set up the ingredients on a table so everyone could serve themselves. There was no coffee.

Brad was irritated. "Why is there never any coffee?" he asked Mariam.

"Nobody ever brings any," she answered.

"I guess I'll just have to."

"Don't forget to bring enough for everyone."

"What? That's a hell of a lot of coffee. It'd be too heavy."

"That's probably why no one brings coffee, besides the difficulty of keeping it real hot."

"Damn!"

Their entrance into Johann-Most Island Harbor was an *Event*, or at least it seemed so to Brad. There was much tooting of horns by the crew of the Glockenspiel, and ringing of bells by those on land. Passengers began leaning against the bow rail and waving to people on shore. There was cheering from those on land and giddy excitement — expressed as screeching and aimless careening about — from the children among the passengers. So the twice-weekly boat from Gondwana to Most Island entered the harbor, horns blaring, bells ringing, and decorative pennants flying.

Brad was amazed at the welcome Mariam received from her relatives who had come out to the pier where they docked. They were warm and joyful, and everyone kissed everyone else. A woman old enough to be past child-bearing on Earth — who would have probably been employed as a housekeeper in another Family Dome — hugged Mariam with a great show of delight. Brad felt left out. Family "reunions" on Earth were never that raucous, loving, and emotional. And of course they never included women.

Holding him by the sleeve of the hooded jacket she had given him, Mariam said to her greeters, "This is Brad

Darsen, whom I am showing round. He's from Earth. Brad, these are my parents: my father, Harry Sheildsgreen from Harper's Ferry Island, and my mother, Grace Rosenberg from Bolivar Island. And this is my little sister, Rosalie Luxemburg, who was born right here on Most Island, as I was." Brad saw the *'little'* sister as completely nubile, just the right age to be sold into marriage. He smiled at them all, trying to be gracious in a 'family' situation very foreign to him. The variety of skin colour among them was surprising. Both of Mariam's parents were darker than she was. *How can that be?* he wondered.

The family home was on top of a bluff overlooking the harbor. No one but Brad was breathless when they reached the top. Mariam put her arm around his waist and said, "You've led too sedentary a life, Brad, I'll bet, being carried everywhere by machines, sitting down all day studying history, and then that damage from the chlorine gas….."

"Woo ... hoo —" he puffed; "You're probably right, Mariam."

Dinner that night, around a large family table, with several guests in attendance, was a combination of a stir-fried dish made by Harry, Mariam's father, who was the family cook, and other vegetable and rice dishes which Mariam's mother and sister had picked up freshly cooked that afternoon at the food dispensary in Luxemburg Village. The fine flavor of the food was up to the excellent standards Brad – without stopping to analyze why – had come to expect on Kayoss.

Most of the guests were old childhood friends of

Mariam's. One – who was introduced as Fifikk Luxemburg, a Gaapel who was Mariam's oldest friend from toddler-school – was a very skinny non-human with two legs, two arms, and one head with a very thin nose which seemed to be mostly twin nostrils set flat in the face between large eyes above the short hooked beak of an avian predator. Brad found the strange, ugly, alien face revolting.

"Of course the Gaapel mature faster than humans, being born more fully formed from their eggs –" Harry said.

"Yes, we do," squeaked Fifikk, feather-like growths standing up like a faint cloud on hir round head and skinny arms.

"He was always challenging me in school to a race of one kind or another!" Mariam laughed. "He always said we humans are too slow, having evolved from primates, not birds as the Gaapel did!"

He? thought Brad, fighting nausea. *I wonder if she experimented with sex with <u>him</u> when they were children together!* The thought of it filled him with fury. A red haze of jealousy swam before his eyes, and he was afraid he would vomit up the good food he had eaten, or lose consciousness, or worse. *When I am Viceroy, those disgusting alien males will never be allowed near our women!* he thought.

"The rivalry has continued to this day, for we will each captain one of the two finest sloops in the regatta this coming weekend," Fifikk squeaked, hopping up and down on his seat on his skinny legs and splayed three-toed feet.

Dimly, through his haze, he heard Mariam ask him, "Brad, are you all right?"

"Yes, okay," he mumbled. "Getting used to all these aliens at once is hard —"

"Oh, Brad. Take a deep breath."

He felt her warm, loving hand on his back. Brad took a deep breath and did feel better.

"We'll go out together alone on the Falcon tomorrow," Mariam said quietly to him.

"Ha! You see? She names her sloop after an earth-bird!" Fifikk crowed. "We will see if that fake wooden and canvas bird can beat a *real* bird come this next weekend! Awkk, awkk."

"Fifikk, settle your feathers," Mariam's mother said quietly. "Please do not get everyone upset while we are trying to digest our food after dinner."

"Yes, I apologize, Mother." The Gaapel said "Mother" as if it were an honored title. In Fifikk's native language, "Mother" meant "The One who Patiently Warms the Eggs of the Future," a most important job in their culture, which either of their two genders could perform, and thereby earn the title of "Mother."

"Dad, could we have coffee after dinner?" Mariam asked.

"Eh? Certainly. I've got a pot brewing in the kitchen."

"Come on, Brad," Mariam said, almost lifting him out of his chair by pulling on one arm. "Let's get people some coffee."

Brad followed her into the kitchen. While she got cups and saucers down from a cupboard, he leaned shaking against a counter.

"You *are* upset, aren't you?" she asked him.

"Did you ever? ... with him, that bird ... like you and me? . . . uh. . . . ?"

"No, Brad," she said softly, putting her arms around him. "Some people like to communicate sexually with certain types of aliens, but I don't. *Men* are the most alien taste I have. Don't worry."

"Oh, good" he gasped. "I don't think —"

"The coffee urn is behind you. Put some coffee in those cups, would you? I'll get cream and sugar, and a tray."

*   *   *

The next day, Mariam and Brad spent the day alone together on the vast ocean in a small sailboat, which Mariam said was called a sloop, because of the one mast, the number and triangular shape of the sails, and the fore-and-aft-rigging, whatever that meant. Brad had never felt the need to memorize the words or ideas for things which proles or bots had always taken care of. A low-tech, wind-powered boat fit into that category as far as he was concerned.

However, he did quickly learn a few things which had immediate survival value for him. Whenever she called out, "Ready About! Hard a-lee!" he knew to duck, so he did not get hit in the head by the boom which swung quickly in the wind from one side of the boat to the other, while he crossed over to the other side so he would not be dumped in the water when the sloop heeled over on its new tack. He was surprised at how much fun it was to "hike" out on the windward side of the boat — which Mariam explained was the direction from which the wind was coming — to counter-balance the push of the wind which would tip the boat over if they did not "hike." The rush of the wind and the slap of the seawater against the bottom of the boat as they sped along were thrilling in a way he had never known. And while he was so busy ducking the boom, he did not have time to notice how large the ocean was.

"Ready About!" she called. Mariam looked puffy and not at all sexy in her fat yellow life-jacket. "Hard-a-lee!"

He ducked under the swinging boom and scrambled to the other side of the boat to counterbalance the strong push of the wind which always seemed on the verge of pushing them over.

"What if a gust of wind tips us over?" he yelled.

"We fall in the water! That's why I made you wear a life-jacket!" she yelled back at him as the boat rammed its way through a bigger than usual wave, covering them both with cold saltwater spray.

They made it through that most unusual day for Brad without getting any wetter than that spray made them. When he had time to notice — while on a long tack without the boat changing direction — he found himself unafraid of the vastness of the ocean, because he was alone with Mariam and she was obviously a good sailor. Later, as they came up to the buoy where the boat had been moored in the island's harbor, she dropped the sails, and let the friction of the water against the hull slow them to a stop within easy reaching distance of the buoy. Then they climbed into the rowboat they had used to get to the buoy, and Mariam rowed them back to the main pier, since Brad could not get the hang of it, having never been in a rowboat before.

Brad was exhausted that evening, and was barely able to finish his dinner before he staggered to the bed he was sharing with Mariam, and collapsed, glad she seemed not to be expecting sex.

Later, he woke, alone, and got up to empty his bladder. Returning to the bed, he lay listening to fragments of conversation, which included Mariam's voice, from the front porch:

"..... when Andy ....."

".....planning .... two girls ..... two boys ..... like twins ....." (Mariam's voice.)

"Which .... older? ....."

"The girls ..... still patriarchal ...." (Mariam's voice again.)

"..... Brad?"

Brad came fully awake and listened closely for a few minutes, but he heard nothing else he could connect to himself. The murmurs seemed to get lower in volume as he drifted back to sleep.

The next day, and the two days after that, were a wonderful vacation for Brad from the decision he knew he would have to make soon about whether or not to abandon his life in the Family and stay on Kayoss, or use the assault-bots he knew were awaiting him at Alpha Centauri. He put the problem aside and enjoyed the time with Mariam, roaming the cultivated countryside around Luxemburg Village, picking berries, the vast shinning ocean always visible from the top of any hill. All of his exposed skin, sunburned from their day together out on the ocean, was covered with vitamin-E-enriched sunburn cream. Miriam was already tanned to a warm coffee-with-cream colour. They both carried plastic buckets in which to collect berries — Mariam told him what they were picking were berries indigenous to Kayoss, artificially mutated a century ago to suit human stomachs and biochemical systems. "We call them roddenberries," she said. At the end of each wonderfully lazy, warm day, they delivered their berries to the village food-dispensary to be baked into pies and tarts and shared with the entire village.

On their last day together, they spent most of their time in a "secret hideaway" surrounded by thick shrubbery, on her wool blanket, making love slowly and tenderly for a long, timeless, wonderful afternoon. Mariam said she was glad no one else was using it that day, because the "secret hideaway" was known to all the young people of the village, and probably remembered by most of the older people. They had left their berry buckets in the only passageway into the 'hideaway,' as the signal agreed on for generations to not disturb the lovers who had gotten there first.

That was the day, both of them drenched in sunlight, that Brad chose to notice Mariam had a square bandaid-like patch on the skin of her belly above her pubic hair. "What's this?" he asked.

"It's an anti-fertility patch. We don't need an unwanted pregnancy," she said calmly.

Brad was instantly angry. "What?! You seek to subvert giving me a son?" he snapped.

"Well, we're just getting to know one another, and I

knew you weren't trained to prevent spermatogenesis, and we haven't discussed —"

"You couple with me! And yet you seek to prevent the natural, God-given consequence of our union?"

"Sex doesn't always need to result in babies; sometimes it's just for fun or loving communication." she said reasonably.

Brad was made furious by her calm. Didn't she understand the importance of this? Was she so far removed from her natural life as a woman she meant to avoid it altogether and pretend she was a man in all things? "God made you to have babies!" he screamed at her. "That is what you are *for!*"

"I am not a household appliance!" she shouted back at him, pushing herself further away from him on the blanket.

"You are what I say you are! You are my woman!"

Mariam took a deep breath to calm herself down. "Brad, we were hoping you would be able to abandon your bourgeois sense of ownership if you stayed here on Kayoss long enough with us, and came to like us."

"We? Who is *we?*"

"All of us. You don't think we would unthinkingly let an aggressive, Capitalist human being visit our planet without keeping an eye on him and trying to get him to understand the beauty of our freedom, do you?"

"Beauty? Freedom? What are you talking about? No one is free unless he can afford to buy what he wants."

"You're an anthropologist? Can't you understand that different cultures have different paradigms?" she asked.

"Of course. But my research has taught me that *my*

society, the United Families of Earth, is the best culture the human species has ever produced. Advanced Capitalism as an economic system is the pinnacle of civilization, obviously."

"Obviously? An economic system in which the vast majority of the human species must live with unrelenting, backbreaking toil; lousy or non-existent medical care; poor or inadequate housing; bad food; short, brutish lives; and —"

"Survival of the fittest still applies," he snapped. "The human race has been considerably improved by the competition of Capitalism. The best survive and prosper. The losers die and don't reproduce. There's no point in arguing against the clear reality of the basic competitive nature of the Race of Man, and how superior men always win out over inferior ones."

"So being sexist, racist, anti-Semitic, and classist are survival traits?"

"Of course. The inferiority of women, Darkies, Jews, all non-Christians, and losers in the game of Capitalism is obvious, and needs no intellectual defense."

"Brad, your thinking is so rigid. Can't you understand that 'survival of the fittest' applies to human *cultures* as well as to individual members of any species of animals or plants? Capitalism is an economic culture which, unlike successful animal species, fouls its own nest. That is why Earth is dying. The practice of Capitalism is killing it."

"It doesn't matter. We have the best of the old biosphere preserved in our Domes, and we will be able to go from Earth out into the Galaxy, where, among a hundred billion stars, there will be ones with planets we can use to recreate the old pre-industrial Earth of our ancestors. We now know enough to keep dirty industry out in Space, not on the surface of a livable planet. Since we've broken that damned Barrier the aliens put up, nothing can stop us now."

"What if those other planets already have a sapient civilization upon them?"

"Doesn't matter. Man is superior, and will take what he wants from nature, on Earth, or anywhere in the galaxy."

Shaking her head with sorrow, knowing their brief, passionate, fun-filled affair was over, Mariam said, "Brad, we had so hoped that living here on Kayoss with us for a little while would change the cultural assumptions you make about human beings who do not conform to your preconceived notions of how people ought to behave. Now, I suppose you are going to go home and come back with an invasion fleet. Will you *force* us to conform to your view of human society? How many of us will die when you come to make our world over to your specifications?"

"Only those who resist." He was lying. He did not intend to house or feed those who were of no use to him.

"I see," she said, bouncing to her feet. "I thought I could see a better man beneath your Capitalist bravado, a man who could learn how to live as an equal with other human beings, a man who could learn how to be truly happy. But I see now I was wrong. Goodbye, Brad." Gathering-up her clothes, she left the hideaway, running easily over the hills to Luxemburg Village to find someone of her own sort to talk to about the problem they were all now facing. She knew Brad would go back to Earth and return with an invasion fleet, now that he felt betrayed by a woman who had made her own free, adult choice about pregnancy.

Brad ran after her, out of the hideaway. He watched her run — berry-bucket in hand — up the hill away from him, over the top, and out of his sight. He picked up his own berry bucket as he went back into the "secret hideaway." He looked at the wool blanket where he and Miriam had made love. He could think of nothing except that Mariam had refused to give him a son. She had secretly killed his sperm – *his* sperm – the messenger of Life. She had deliberately caused him to spill his Seed on fallow ground. That was a *sin,* a terrible sin. Screeching in pain, Brad picked up the wool blanket and threw it at the bushes surrounding him. Breathing hard through clenched teeth, he flailed at the blanket and the bushes with his bucket until he tore off the plastic handle.

Two women, their arms around each other's waists, came into the hideaway at that moment. One of them said, "Oh, sorry. There was nothing in the entranceway. So we —"

Pushing the thought, and the sight of the two of them, out of his mind, Brad quickly left the "secret hideaway," mumbling misogynist epithets to himself: "Fucking bitch, filthy cunthole. . . ."

These damned proles need to be _ruled_. They let their females act like _people_, neglecting their God-ordained womanly-duty to nourish the Seed of Men. I'll teach them, when I'm Viceroy. I _will_ be Viceroy. I can't let those damned squishy aliens rule them any longer. This will be _my_ planet, _my_ proles, and _my_ females, to do with as I please!

There was a local alcoholic beverage with dinner that night, and since strong drink had never been part of his life on Earth, Brad, trying to numb his sudden psychic pain, drank too much of the delicious, strong, homemade wine. Avoiding even looking at Miriam's sad, distant face, he became more inebriated than he had ever been in his life, and was unable to guard his tongue. After dinner, he asked Mariam's father if he could speak with him alone, so Harry led him into the small family library beside the dining room.

"Uh, Harry, I've been thinking a lot about it, and I want to keep your daughter Miriam. Now, I'll be away for a while, bringing in the Darsen assault-bots –"

"*Assault*-bots?"

"Oh, don't worry. No real violence will be necessary, I'm sure, once people see that a man has come from Earth, the cradle of Mankind, to rescue them from the grip of the aliens, and bring them the freedom of Capitalism, which can make you all rich, or at *least* all of you who have a good business sense, and work hard to make your fortunes. I'll see to it that you and your family come to no harm –"

"*Freedom* of Capitalism?"

"Oh, I admit that *advanced* Capitalism, as we have it on Earth, leaves little room for individuals not of the Families to become successful entrepreneurs —"

"Successful —"

"But you'll be in on the ground floor when we start up Capitalism on this planet. The economy will be looser, with the wealth of unexploited resources this planet has, and with the starter money I'll give you for Mariam and her sister, and the ingenuity I'm sure you possess, or your girls would not be so bright —"

"My girls —"

"And don't worry about not having any sons! When the Families are in power here, and you are in good shape financially, you can buy yourself another wife, a teenager, like Rosalie, to give you the sons your old wife couldn't give you before Capitalism came to rescue you and your manhood. If necessary, as Viceroy, I'll give you a special dispensation —"

"What?"

"Of course, I want to buy Mariam for my wife. I know she's a bit old, but I . . . *I like her.* And if you let me buy Rosalie too, then they both can get started right away growing me sons to be born on this new planet of mine. . . . We'll build a beautiful femhouse for your girls to be safe and secure in. Don't worry. What I pay you for them will greatly benefit your Family —"

"*Pay* me? —"

"Surely, you cannot pretend that without Capitalism, you are ***prospering*** in the midst of this ridiculous ***anarkhy*** the aliens have imposed on you where there is no opportunity for an enterprising man to get ahead of the crowd and make an affluent, powerful life for himself —"

"Affluent? Powerful?"

"You can be the Founder of the Sheildsgreen Family on Kayoss. How about that?"

"Founder?"

"Of course it's coming. It is inevitable now that the Families have discovered you."

"Families?"

"The Darsen Family is the best. And you'll all be glad to get out from under the thumb — oops! the pseudopods — of the Geejjikk, those damned squishy aliens, so smug to be speaking English, the glorious language of White men —"

"White men —"

"Yes, there are enough of you to make a superior class of humans, and a little colour won't matter, like you have — obviously you're mostly White or your daughters wouldn't be so pale. You just tan dark, 'n need to stay out of the sun —"

"Superior? —"

"After the Families come to Kayoss, you will have a real *human* civilization, within the genius of Capitalism. You won't be pets of aliens anymore, forced to live with them and perform for them, and pretend they are socially your equals. None of that nonsense —"

"Nonsense —"

"Yes. You'll have a dynamic economy, a chance for the best of you to use your aggressive human nature and your bartering skills to build a rich life for yourselves and contribute to the advancement of your species. Capitalism will make all of you *really free*. With the money you make you can create a genuinely rich way of life for everyone, where the work of a man's mind or hands will raise him up to a truly civilized level, a wealthy human level, where no one can look down on him, where he won't have to kow-tow to aliens, '*taking care*' *of them* when they invade and contaminate private human amusements, like basketball games —"

"Aliens—"

"You, know, Mariam suggested I could stay here and get a job teaching at a university. But now, I realize it is my duty to rescue you people from your alien owners, those Geejjikk, who are obviously running the show here, twisting your minds, pretending to be affable, warm-hearted benefactors, letting your females pretend to be people —"

"Rescue?"

"When I'm Viceroy, I can teach a course at any one of your universities. It will be very popular: *The History of Capitalism and the Liberty of Man*, taught by your Viceroy. How great that will be!"

THE PRICE OF FREEDOM

Drunk enough to be blissfully unaware of his surroundings – and immersed in the warm glow of his own fantasies of success, having solved the problem of Mariam and her un-womanly ways— Brad staggered to the bed he had shared with Mariam, barely noticing she was not there.

The next morning he awoke with a blazing headache. He had heard of hangovers, but he had never had one before. Mariam was not in bed with him. In his pajamas, he stumbled down to the breakfast table.

Harry put a bread-loaf-shaped plastic box next to Brad's placemat.

"What?" Brad asked.

"That's a loaf of banana bread, to take back to Dr. Steve

at the West-Mikhail Healing Clinic and Trauma Center," Harry said.

Brad put the plastic box in his backpack, took two strong pain pills from a bottle therein, and then looked around the table. "Where's Mariam?" he asked.

"Gone," Harry said.

"What?" Brad asked.

"Gone, back to Mikhail Village. Conceded her part in the race to Fifikk. Took the bi-weekly boat back to Gondwana. Late last night."

"Oh, all right. Why did Mariam leave? A medical emergency?"

"Nope."

"Then why? *Why?*"

"Finished with you, I think. She heard us talking last night. Doesn't want to be your property. Doesn't want to lose our Anarkhy. Says you are incapable of — how did she put it? —You are 'not capable of transcending your cultural bias.' Told me to tell you to talk to William. Fortunately, there's another boat back to Bakunin Village three days from now."

"No!" Brad screamed, standing up abruptly and knocking over his chair. "Why did you let her leave? Can't you *control* your females?"

"She's a free person. Brad," Harry said calmly, raising an eyebrow in his wife's direction.

"You damned prole!" Brad was shaking with frustration and rage. "I was a fool to think any of you could ever be anything else! Pussy-whipped losers!" Brad leaped away from the table, slammed open the glass doors to their dining terrace, and ran down the hill to the village pier. It was empty.

He looked out west across the ocean and screamed, "Mariam! Mariam!" He fell to his knees, and howling, hit himself repeatedly on the front of his thighs. Then he lay over on his side and rolled around on the bare wood of the pier, moaning, "No, no ..." over and over. Harry and Grace — who had run down the hill after him — stopped him from rolling off the pier into deep water. He fought them as though they were trying to harm him, and ran off howling through the clean early-morning streets of the village, up into the hills above.

Harry, Grace and other people of Luxemburg Village could see the severe psychological pain Brad was in, but they did not know how to help him. Over the next two days they sporadically watched him from a distance as he wandered the hills above the village, in his rumpled pajamas, talking to himself and grazing, apparently unconsciously, on ripe roddenberries.

In the night between the two days, he slept where he fell. He was in no danger. The only animals on Most Island were those brought from Earth, and the villagers kept their billy goats penned up. Their llamas were too pleasant-tempered to bother anyone.

In late afternoon of the second day, Brad accidentally re-discovered the leafy entrance to the "secret hideaway" he had briefly shared with Mariam. He stumbled over three berry-buckets on his way in.

Occupying the hideaway were three men, two dark and

one pale, obviously mis-using their genitals, committing the heinous perversion of sodomy with each other. They were very noisily enjoying themselves.

Shocked beyond endurance, Brad vomited half-digested roddenberries — and several small indigenous-to-Kayoss leaves edged in pink, which would have made him very sick if they had been in his stomach long enough to break down into their poisonous components — and he ran screaming from what to him was an horrific scene.

The nausea reminded him of an incident which had happened when he was a boy: An older teenaged cousin of his, Brandon Darsen, had been found committing sodomy with another boy. The Darsen Family justice had been appropriate and swift. If he could not use his genitals properly, he could not have them. Brad had been assigned with an older cousin to hold down Brandon's right leg, while other cousins held down his other limbs, and the boy's uncle – Brad's father – sat on his chest to grab the boy's entire genitals in his big left hand, and cut them off using a dull serrated knife. Brad had been splattered with blood, and had vomited on the wound. Remembering, he could still hear the boy screaming . . .

On Most Island, not looking where he was going as he ran, Brad fell down a hill onto a deserted beach beside the sea. He lay senseless on the warm sand, trying not to re-live hearing the boy's shrill screams. He twisted deeper into the sand and mercifully fell asleep.

The tide coming in after sundown woke him up. Consumed with a desire to exercise his manhood, he climbed the hill beside him, until he could see the top of the bluff where Mariam's family house sat.

He waited patiently, cross-legged in the dark, until all the lights in Mariam's house went out, one after another; telling him everyone had gone to bed.

He stopped on the front porch to listen if anyone was still awake, and then he entered the house easily, because *all the doors were unlocked.* The stupid proles trusted that no stranger would enter to rob them or hurt them. They were contemptuous.

Brad found his way easily in the dim light to Rosalie's room. That door was also unlocked. *Harry hasn't the sense to lock up his most valuable possession!*

Her luscious teenaged femaleness was a shapely lump beneath the sheet. Standing beside Rosalie's bed, he gazed down on her delicious womanly body. She looked like a younger Mariam. His manhood rising, Brad whipped the sheet off and leaped upon her, pushing her over on her back, forcing her thighs open with his knees. She woke up startled, and tried to push him away, shouting, "No! No!" And then screaming as he thrust into her. *Damned dry bitch,* he thought, hitting her in the face with his fist, to silence her. He heard and felt the crack as her nose broke. It didn't matter. It would not interfere with her fertility.

As far as he was concerned, he was only doing what he had a God-given right to do. He had conveniently forgotten he was on another planet where the rules were different. On Earth, all the laws supported his assumptions of male entitlement, and he had come to believe those laws were the laws of the universe. They were God's laws, impossible to break without destroying civilization. After all, little Rosalie belonged to no Family Man, so he was free to take her as he chose. She was *only a female*. Only a *prole*-female.

He closed his eyes so he couldn't see her agonized face, closed his ears to her ridiculous screams, and concentrated on his own pleasure . . . *ah, good, fuck . . . fuck . . .* thinking of his sons to come, all with Mariam's curly auburn hair, all *his sons* because he would be the Viceroy of Kayoss, renamed the planet Darsen. . . .

Rough hands pulled him off her. "Hey! What? Stop, I'm not finished!" he cried.

Harry, Grace, and several adult overnight guests threw Brad out a partially closed window. He landed on the porch roof among broken wood and shards of glass, slashing a forearm, an elbow, and a shoulder. He rolled off the roof and landed on some thorny rose bushes. Naked, covered with blood, Brad ran away down the hill to the Luxemburg Harbor pier, afraid his life was in danger.

The usual response of Anarkhists on Kayoss to the rare, socially unacceptable behavior of forcing sex on an unwilling person was to exile the rapist from the society of decent people, and to suggest he run to a sanctuary staffed with mental-health professionals to avoid being maimed or killed by the outraged family and friends of the person he had sexually attacked.

When Rosalie's rescuers followed Brad down the hill, they could see he did not understand the seriousness of his mistake. He refused to hear them when they told him to see a mind-mender for his anti-social behavior. Rather than beat Brad to a pulp, which was what Rosalie's father, Harry, wanted to do — he did manage to crack one of Brad's ribs when he kicked him — the group's main concern was in getting Rosalie immediately to the Most Island Healing Clinic.

So, throwing his backpack and his clothes at him — *"Get off our island, you piece of shit!"* — they left Brad on the pier, curled around the agony of his broken rib. He lay in pain all that night, remembering his times with Mariam: sliding into her, sliding into her, sliding into her, sliding into her, walking beside her, listening to the many things she said:

"There is only <u>one</u> human race, Brad."

"You have nothing to pack. We have better things to do with our morning, hmmm?"

"We have to take care of these Ttiiffsts. Here, hold on like this."

"Please help us with these Djuiivv, Brad."

"Ready about! Hard a-lee!"

"Brad."

"Brad?"

"Brad!"

"I am <u>not</u> a household appliance!"

If only she had not contrived to rob him of a son.

*   *   *

The boat from Gondwana docked late that morning, noisily as usual. Irritated, Brad found the repetitious, "spontaneous" celebration of the boat's arrival disgusting. He boarded the boat and sat in the bow with his back to the railing, his eyes slitted with pain — watching the horrible proles, all the shades of dark he had to share the boat with — holding himself together with great effort, in limbo until he could reach his spaceship, get to Alpha Centauri, and thereby fulfill his obligations to his Family, his *real* human Family, those who were not darkies, not *pets* to the damned squishy aliens. . . .

Hours later, mid-ocean, Brad groped in the backpack William Johnbrown had gifted him so long ago, and found the plastic box of banana bread Harry had given him to deliver to Mariam's doctor friend. Uncomfortably hungry, he ate much of it, unsurprised at how tasty it was. All the food he had eaten on Kayoss had been delicious. He did not stop to consider that human beings who like to cook – especially if they are given the best ingredients possible, without regard to "price" – make the best cooks of all. That was something even a well-programmed bot could not duplicate with the foodstuffs available in the Darsen Domes. He threw over his shoulder overboard into deep salt water what he had not managed to eat. *I am no damned messenger-bot,* he thought.

He stayed awake the entire trip, unwilling to admit to himself he was frightened of the proles around him, who no longer seemed so harmless and unthreatening. When they docked at the Bakunin Harbor pier, he ran from the boat, his demons chasing him; running until the pain in his bloody slashes and punctures, and in his cracked rib, stopped him.

He was lost. He recognized none of the buildings. Without large advertising signs or neon, he could not tell if he was among factories, dormitories, or dispensing stores. He tried to raise his fists above his head, but the pain from his broken rib prevented him. So he stood with his hands at his side and screamed, "Where is the Skyhook? The Skyhook! The Skyhook!"

One three-legged orange-ish creature and several humans stopped to give him directions. He listened to the human with the lightest skin colour, didn't bother to thank anyone, and walked in the direction they had all been pointing.

He found the plaza in front of the Skyhook entrance soon enough. The fountain full of shameless naked children of indeterminate genders was still there, and he located the brick path to the inn where he had first stayed in Mikhail Village.

At the inn, he climbed stairs, his side and his lacerations still bothering him, to the room where he had shared space with William, and found a group of darkie-proles who told him they had been using that room for a week. Rushing two flights down to the lobby, he charged the intake desk and aggressively demanded to know where William Johnbrown had gone. He leaned wearily against the desk, pain evident in his face.

The deskclerk, beardless and wearing a baggy smock, was apparently unflappable. (He?)(She?) said, "Brother, you look terrible. Are you sick? Hurt? There's a healing clinic not far away. Can I call you an ambulance?" (he?)(she?) asked in an androgynous tone of voice.

"No! No ambulance! I need to find William Johnbrown. Where is he?" Brad gasped.

"What's he look like?" the (man?)(woman?) asked.

"About my height. Good-looking, young, strawberry-blond mustache, head hair to match, always wears a green t-shirt, plays a wooden flute, a good cook. Uh, I really need to find him."

"Have a seat, please. Lie down on that sofa over there. I'll call round the inn and see if anyone remembers him. Just relax. We'll find your friend."

Brad followed the suggestion and lay down on the couch. He was too tired to be frightened. He needed to see William's almost-Earth-normal, friendly face. He fell asleep, fitfully, tortured by images of Mariam running away from him. He tried to catch her in his dreams and tell her he was sorry he had broken her nose, but first she had to realize he needed a son . . . *a son.*

"Hey, Brother?"

"Zzzz-huh?" Brad opened his eyes.

The desk clerk – still not identifiable as either a man or a woman – and a bearded man wearing a stained apron, stood beside the couch where Brad was stretched out. The deskclerk said, "Jay de-Santillan here knows William Johnbrown," pointing hir thumb at the man in the apron.

"Oh! Great," Brad said, trying to sit up, but failing. "Where is he? How do you know him?" he asked weakly.

"I met him when he helped out in the kitchen here," Jay said. "He and his partner work out of Chomsky Station, as tourist-guides for strangers who come to Kayoss. He went

177

back up-orbit a week ago. Did you meet him at our local kemmerhouse?'

"Huh? No. I'm a visitor. He was my guide for a while."

"He lives in First Village in Chomsky. You know he'll be glad to see you. He's a really friendly fellow. We love him at the kemmerhouse, when he's here," Jay said, grinning broadly.

"Let's give him a call," the desk clerk said, heading off to the desk and activating a comscreen. (He?)(She?) returned shortly, saying, "He'll pick you up at the Skyhook station in Chomsky day-after-tomorrow morning. All you have to do is catch the Skyhook today, in a few hours. Meanwhile, here's somebody –"

"Hi, I'm Kent Audrelorde," a brown young man in blue shorts and a yellow t-shirt said, stepping up to sit beside Brad on the couch. "I'm an apprentice-doctor at the local healing clinic here. Since we can't get you to become an official patient, why don't you tell me what the problem is, and I'll do what I can to make you feel better. You look like you've been sick and in a lot of pain for quite a while now."

"I need to catch the Skyhook," Brad whispered hoarsely.

"Of course. Now, tell me where it hurts."

Ignoring the prole-doctor's skin colour, pretending the man was only deeply tanned, and speaking to him as if he were a regular person, Brad said, "My side hurts. I think I have a broken rib."

"Where? Show me."

Brad pulled up his shirt and showed his injured side.

"That's quite a bruise. Does it hurt real bad?"

"Yes."

"Real, *real* bad?"

"Yes, damnit. I said it does. No! Don't touch it!" Brad screeched.

"Yep. Probably broken. Are you coughing up any blood or having trouble breathing"

"No."

"Good. Now, let me listen to your heart and lungs. I won't go near your bruised side. I have my stethoscope right here. I always carry it round my neck. I'm so proud to be an apprentice-doctor, you see." He smiled, his teeth flashing white in his dark face.

Typical darkie smile, Brad thought, leaning his head back and closing his eyes, shutting out the world and its pain.

The apprentice put the earpieces in his ears and listened intently with first the bell and then the diaphragm of his stethoscope to Brad's heart beating steadily, perhaps a bit too fast, and to his lungs, which seemed a little raspy, but with no bloody gurgling. "Okay," he said, standing up, moving the stethoscope from his ears to around his neck, and returning the bell / diaphragm end to his chest pocket. "Thanks for letting me practice on you. Now we'll —"

"Practice?" Brad said, alarmed.

"Hey, Brother," the deskclerk broke in, "if you're not going to go to the clinic, it can't hurt you to let him practice with his stethoscope. Anything else he does he's had lots of experience with, right?" The clerk raised (his?)(her?) eyebrows at the apprentice.

"Right," Kent said. "Now, we'll bind your upper torso with tape, so that broken rib won't move around and poke a hole in your lungs or your heart. We'll patch up these bloody lacerations and punctures you have too. You'll see a full doctor up-orbit, won't you? To check my bandaging? And the harshness of your breathing?"

"Okay," Brad answered. He had made it so far. The tape probably wouldn't hurt him. He had seen it done to a cousin of his who had stopped a fast ball when he was up to bat and had broken a rib.

*   *   *

William met him at the Skyhook station, and took him in an elevator — in which their weight gradually increased — to the Station's living section, the inner curve of the spinning "tin can" which was Chomsky Station, six miles in diameter and twenty miles long.

"Here we are," William said, waving his arms to show off the amazingly verdant vista of the Station's interior. They were standing on a concrete terrace on a low hill outside the elevator, which enabled them to see through remarkably clear air to the center dividing wall of the "can." It was ten miles away, behind which was a CO_2-rich environment where most of the Station's grains and vegetables were grown, tended by the CO_2-loving Djuiivvs. "You see, up there" – William pointed overhead to the left – "is Second Village, about six miles plus, or one hundred twenty degrees around the curve from where we're standing." Brad looked up, squinting his eyes against the glare from the suntube, a twenty-mile long nanobot-manufactured diamond tube running along the axis of the spinning "can," which brought in sunlight to light the interior of the "can" with mirrors on the "south pole" angled to shine light from Che, the sun, directly into the suntube. "And over there" – William pointed overhead and to the right – "is Third Village, a quarter more than six miles further around, and" – he continued, pointing – "down the hill there, that's First Village, where I live with my partner. Come on."

Brad mentioned that he needed to see a doctor, so they stopped in the First Village Sapient Clinic & Veterinary Hospital. A human doctor there listened to his lungs, and pronounced Brad's taped ribs and bandaged lacerations "as good a job as can be done. Just come back again tomorrow afternoon for another check-up. Okay?"

"All right," Brad answered, thinking to himself, *To hell with it. I've got enough pain pills to last me. I'll be gone tomorrow to Alpha Centauri! I'm sick of these damned proles!*

*   *   *

At William's house, on the back terrace outside his kitchen, the two friends sat and sipped coffee; Brad, gritting his teeth and throttling his rage, explained to William what had happened with Mariam.

"Oh, my," William said. "That does get into those subjects we agreed not to talk about: *women* and *reproduction?* Doesn't it?"

"I just don't see how your so-called civilization can *survive,* letting your females decide when to get pregnant. What woman would agree to go through all the trouble, the discomfort, the inconvenience of pregnancy, and the pain of childbirth, unless she was *required* to?"

"Okay, so we *will* talk about it," William sighed. "As a man, I admit I'm always surprised that women willingly and eagerly get pregnant and have babies. I sure wouldn't want to. And I am especially grateful when two fine women like Mariam Luxemburg and Andrea Bakunin ask me to be seedfather to their kids."

"What?" Brad slammed down his coffee mug and stood up, clenching his fists, ready for a fight.

"Sit down, Brad. I'm not gonna fight you. It's time you faced a few facts about life, and about women, here in our Anarkhist culture of Kayoss."

"What?"

"Mariam was having an affair with you for the *fun* of it. And you *did* have fun, didn't you?"

"Yes, but she shouldn't have been allowed to avoid giving me a son."

"So you wanted the fun, as long as *only the woman* had to face the consequences of your mutual fertility."

"But that is what women are *for!*"

"Hold on. Hold on. First of all, Brad, *women are people,* no matter how many laws you've passed on Earth to try and make them *things.* Human beings —- and I include women in that category —- have an instinct for freedom, and we humans can never be enslaved forever."

"No! Freedom is a commodity, like everything else. You can't have it if you can't pay for it."

"Yes, that's the basic Capitalist view, isn't it? Marx taught us that sooner or later, in Capitalism, *everything becomes a commodity.* We saw that happen in Earth history. Food became a commodity; water, heat, even decent air. Housing, health-care, education, even just access to information. Everything came to be owned by the bourgeoisie, to be exploited for profit. Everything on Earth has to be paid for – right? – those without money are entitled to nothing except misery and death. And you call that *civilization!*"

"Yes, I do," Brad said stiffly, rejecting Brad's crazy *Anarkhist* and Socialist ideas. "Only those who work are entitled to live. We have the goodness of Earth preserved in our Family Domes, while the damned useless proles wallow outside in filth, as they deserve."

"And you have worked very hard, all your life, for everything you have?" William asked angrily.

"My ancestors did, the ones who founded the Family. And I work, at my profession."

"And the proles are entitled to nothing because their ancestors were Workers, not owners?" William asked.

"That's the harsh logic of history," Brad smirked.

"And a good thing if you were born onto the winning side," William snapped.

"Yes." Brad smiled happily.

"Well, here on Kayoss," William said angrily, "things are different. We have no government, no ruling class. We cooperate with each other as free people, each of us, women included, free to make our *own* decisions about our *own* lives. And let me tell you about Mariam Luxemburg. She and her life-partner, Andrea Bakunin, long ago — when they were apprentice health-care-Worker classmates — met, fell in love, and planned to raise children together.

And since I grew up as an older child on Harper's Ferry Island with Mariam's father, Harry, I was lucky enough —"

"You're as old as Mariam's father?"

"Yes. I told you once it had been a long time since I was twenty earthyears old. I have rejuvenated in a healing-pod every decade since I was thirty. That's four times. I'm sixty-three earthyears old now."

"Oh God."

"And I was around in Luxemburg Village when Mariam was growing up. So, later on, she and Andy asked me to be the sperm donor for their kids, since I'm exclusively homosexual, and Carver and I can't make babies together."

Brad pushed his chair further away from William's, trying to remain calm. "You're a homosexual?" he asked, stumbling to his feet, shuddering with revulsion.

"Yes. That should be obvious to you by now."

"And you have pervert sex with other males? How?"

"Brad, I'm not going to discuss my sex life with you, for heaven's sake."

"And Mariam? How could she? With me?"

"Mariam is bisexual, obviously."

"Then why? How could she? Why does she want a family with another female?"

"She fell in love with Andy first, a long time ago."

"And all these unnatural relationships are tolerated on your world?"

"Not tolerated. Accepted; celebrated."

"That's disgusting." Brad stood up straighter. "Tell me how I can get back to my ship."

"You're leaving? I was hoping you could stay for dinner.

Carver will be home, and Fifikk, the Gaapel you met at Harry's house, will be here also. Long ago, his egg-layer, a friend of mine, left his egg with me. I incubated the egg —"

"What?"

No! Not personal**y**! I mean I used a sunlamp and wrapped the egg in a wool blanket. After the Gaapel hatched, I served as his Mother until he was grown up, when I lived on Most Island before I met Carver. I was delighted with the chance to raise an alien son."

"Perverts! Disgusting proles! Unnatural monsters! Mothers to aliens! Where is my ship? I've got to get away! I want to go home!" Brad shouted, and tried to wave his arms over his head. "Mariam!" he squeaked past the tears and anguish clogging his throat. Where is my ship?" he whispered.

Feeling compassion for Brad's pain, William wanted to put his arms around the Earthman, but he knew it would be misunderstood. So instead, he went into his house and turned down the heat on the electric crock-pot and led Brad up the hill past the Skyhook and the Q-unit to the elevator to the Starport where his ship waited in freefall. Before they parted, William pressed a small phone into Brad's hand, saying "If you need a friend, call me. There are several numbers for me, here in Chomsky and on Kayoss, in the '*store*' area. Just press here, Okay?"

Brad turned angrily away, ignoring William. He never said goodbye. William knew he would never notice that the Chomsky proles who had investigated his ship had fixed his broken G-change alarm. William thought to himself the truth was that Brad would probably *not* have decided to join the Anarkhist society on Kayoss, even if Mariam had been single and willing to get pregnant immediately. *Some people are set in their ways, determined to be unfree and lonely,* he thought.

William went home to finish making dinner for his partner and his alien-son. Brad blasted for the wormhole, once again trusting his safety and his destination to the Darsen bots on his ship.

book four
"CONQUEST"

*　　*　　*

The assault-bots — small, lean robot-spaceships designed solely for wreaking destruction — were waiting for Brad at Alpha-Centauri, giant shiploads of them. The bots were armed with enough incendiary missiles to easily decimate an average rocky planet. There were no nuclear bombs because the Family was smart enough not to irradiate their new property with material which would make the planet uninhabitable for millions or billions of years.

Brad established his human control over the bots crewing his armada, making sure they had been newly programmed to fulfill their function as his invasion force, although he actually had no understanding of their Programming. He could not write code. That was work the Proles were for.

Brad took the Darson Family Assault-bots back through the wormhole to the planet Kayoss, which had no space defense, as far as he knew. *The fools!*

The Darsen Family Armada arrived at the planet of Kayoss less than a week after Brad Darsen had left it. William Johnbrown and the *'ad-hoc-Committee to "Convert" the Capitalist Visitor from Earth'* had believed Brad would have to return to Earth — 4.35 lightyears away

187

from the wormhole connecting the Alpha-Centauri and the Xye'tsst star-systems — at less than the speed of light, in order to report to his superiors and arrange for an invasion fleet. They had believed they had almost nine earthyears to decide what to do to avoid the threat of a violent Capitalist takeover.

They — Professor Davida Louisemichel, Doctors Vladimir Mikhail and Mariam Luxemburg, radio-operator Dana Goldman, homemaker Harry Sheildsgreen, Geep Child-of-Gerr-&-Therp, and their colleagues in the *Committee* — had all been disastrously wrong.

Staring at Chomsky Station, Brad looked at the viewscreen on the bridge of his new flagship. The homosexual William — whom Brad had thought was a regular guy-friend — lived there with his pervert lover, and his alien, ugly bird-son.

Mariam was planning to give William — *a god-damned sodomite!*— a human son. Damn her. She wouldn't give Brad Darsen, her lover, a normal man, a son. *Fuck-ass perverts,* he thought. *Betraying the goodness of manly friendship. They stain the decency of the Race of Man. They foul the memory of successful men and their sons down through the sweep of history!*

They cannot be permitted to continue. They must not be allowed to be part of the glorious Race of Man. He would see to the castration and the execution of all those "male" perverts when he was Viceroy. Women would be forced into femhouses to fulfill their womanly duty to the Race of Man. He would fuck Mariam again, and she would learn the satisfaction of being a normal woman in a great

Capitalist society. She would give him sons. She would learn to be proud she was the first wife of the Viceroy!

Without any orders from Brad, his bot-crewed assault ships suddenly fired on Chomsky Station. It broke apart — silently in the vacuum of Space, in horribly slow motion — like a cheap plastic toy. Over three thousand station Workers, of various species, were suddenly exposed to the cold airlessness of space, many while they slept. *The bots destroyed the Station's irreplaceable Healing Pods, and their secrets of life-extension!*

Brad stared dumbfounded at his viewscreen, shouting into his microphone, "No! Bots! Stop that! A space station is a valuable piece of infrastructure! You are supposed to *invade* it! This is not the Anglo-Asian War on Earth two centuries ago! Do not destroy infrastructure!"

He searched among the exploded corpses still trailing crystallized blood and other bodily fluids, looking for William, his former friend, who had betrayed his manhood, but Brad saw only the mutilated bodies of strange men (and women!) and ugly alien species. He also saw several kinds of eyeballs sprung from their sockets and revolting alien things he couldn't even guess the purpose of. Many of the dead were small enough to be children. He watched a crowd of Djuiivv fly past his viewscreen, looking like ruptured barrels oozing strange organs. Much of the debris from the ruined station fell toward the surface of Kayoss, flaming briefly in friction with the atmosphere.

Rigid with shock and frustration, Brad thought the flames made well-deserved funeral pyres for people who had welcomed perversion and race-mixing into their society. Other pieces — twisted metal, frozen liquids and gases, and the ruined bodies of the many sapient beings who had been the station's crew — exploded outward to the stars, soon lost and immeasurably diluted in the vast abyss of interstellar space.

Imagining the panic on the surface of Kayoss as their space station was so easily destroyed, Brad came to the sick realization that his father had had the bots pre-programmed to start with a spectacular display of blitzkrieg, demonstrating the military power of the Darsen Family. Supposedly — with the inhabitants of Kayoss in a state of shock — the invasion would go much easier after that.

His father had not trusted him. He was only the worthless, expendable youngest son, not enough of a Man —

His father had not trusted him — to personally direct the assault bots to begin the invasion.

His father had not trusted him — to be a strong Man, a conquering General.

Brad thought it should have been done without such overwhelming destruction of resources. Especially the life-extension science. . . .

His father had not trusted him. Obviously, Brad was not thought by anyone in power in his Family to be capable of *any* ruthless, business-like behavior.

In a sudden flash of ice-cold realization, Bard knew without a doubt that the Darsen Family CEO, his great uncle, on the advice of his father — who had never respected or actually cared for him — *would never let him be the Viceroy of any planet,* even one whose resources he alone had catalogued and conquered. He was still the incompetent youngest son of his authoritarian father. The runt of the litter. His love of scholarship had forever labeled him as un-manly and weak. *Damn them.*

It was very quiet on the bridge, the bots whirling quietly at their tasks.

Quiet except for the sound of wracking sobs being forced from a tortured throat. It took him a while to realize it was he himself making such horrible noises.

On orders from his father — against his wishes! — the Darsen assault-bots had just begun to destroy the most interesting culture he had ever seen; and strangely, a culture he had been happy in.

He looked around worriedly, hurriedly — to see who might be watching him, but there were only bots, no human beings, only machines without emotion or personality, no people at all. He was alone. He doubled over with existential loneliness, his guts cramping, as he grabbed his stomach and howled. He wondered why the crying would not go away. With every breath, he croaked in pain. Irritated, he wiped the saltwater from his cheeks.

*   *   *

Suddenly motivated — *he mustn't let the assault bots coming in behind him attack the planet!*

Destroying that brilliantly *human* — the culture <u>was</u> human, he suddenly realized; the aliens were just an interesting minority; the humans were *really, somehow,* in charge of themselves — however strange that might seem to someone raised to believe in meritocratic hierarchy and the basic stupidity of dark-skinned proles —

He must stop the attack on the planet! The Darsen family must not take and destroy the civilization of Kayoss! Damn them (his father and his great-uncle)!

If I can't be Viceroy here, then the Darsen family will never take over! He would never allow his older brothers nor his cousins to be Viceroy and take the woman who was *his.*

He loved Mariam. In all his life as a privileged member of the United Families of Earth, he had never really loved anyone else, he realized. No other man could have her, will have her!

Suddenly decisive, Brad frantically searched his pockets for the phone William had given him, finally finding it in a lower-leg pouch he had forgotten his trousers held. He punched one of the numbers for the surface of Kayoss.

"Hello. Harry Sheildsgreen."

"Hello, hello," Brad said loudly, afraid the man — Rosalie's father, who had broken his rib and tried to kill him — would hang up. "Harry, I've lost control of the assault bots! Without warning, against my orders, they destroyed Chomsky Station. You're all in danger! Do you have any planetary defense?"

"Is this Brad Darsen?" Harry asked coldly. Brad imagined the small phone in his hand had turned into a slim chunk of ice.

"Yes, yes! Please believe me —"

"I have to go now," Harry said, more coldly than before, and he hung up.

Frantic, because he couldn't know whether or not Harry Sheildsgreen believed his warning, or would do anything, Brad called all the numbers in William's phone, even the ones for Chomsky Station, which rang and rang. . . .

Harry put down his phone and turned to his guest, William JohnBrown, who had come down to Kayoss a few days before with his husband Carter and his son Fifikk, because they were worried about what Brad might do, and what the *'ad-hoc-Committee to "Convert" the Capitalist Visitor from Earth'* needed to plan for.

"The Planetary Defense Syndic has been alerted," Harry said to William.

"I worked with them for a while, about thirty years ago. They're well-practiced," William said.

"I always thought those folks had a great job," Harry said. "Flying planes all the time, to practice targeting and shooting-down unauthorized spaceplanes pretending to be potential bio-contaminators breaching our atmosphere; like kids playing a great game, defending Kayoss from foreign proteins, bugs, prions, and viruses we have no natural defenses against. . . ."

"Yes, it was great fun."

"I understand the work of the Defense Syndic gets boring after a while, always practicing on duds," Harry said.

"Sure, but the turnover just guarantees that the current Guardians are all young, enthusiastic people, sharp and happily competent at their jobs."

*   *   *

Since they had expected no effective defense, the Darsen Family Programmers had not written into the assault-bots code clever enough to wage war against a competent and intractable foe. As wave after wave of Darsen-bots attacked the planet, the only damage they were able to inflict on Kayoss was on small, isolated, village communities and their farmlands, on islands surrounded by the vast ocean of Kayoss, far away from where Planetary Defense had flyers, bases and runways.

Planetary Defense — the young people, flyers: women, men, and various aliens, many of them the bird-like Gaapels — threw every resource they had into the fight to repel and eliminate the invading assault-bots of the Darson Family. Glad they supposedly were not shooting-down actual living beings, but rather only military robots belonging to humans who wanted to enslave their planet, the Defense Syndic flyers cheered every time they destroyed an assault-bot and saw it fall to Kayoss, usually into the ocean.

From the bridge of his starship Brad was able —- unimpeded by the bots diligently following their pre-programmed orders —- to access images from long-range cameras pointed at the surface.

Watching from orbit, Brad alternately screamed in pain and cheered in triumph, watching isolated villages laid waste, all their (surprisingly rural!), clean, neat, practical architecture reduced to rubble, but the '*city*' of Skyhook was not being damaged. Planetary Defense had hangers and runways near the '*city*.'

194

So maybe Mariam will live, Brad thought, surprised by his own overwhelming sense of relief, the temporary lift of crushing misery from his heart. *Now she can live*, he thought. *Despite refusing to give me a son. A son with curly auburn hair. H*e mourned the child he would never see, who would never live.

He took a deep breath, in the anguish of his loneliness, loneliness he now fully felt. He was now forever separated from Mariam, destined to never be Viceroy *anywhere*. As long as he chose to live.

He thought to the future — *his* future — a little-regarded member — a *loser*-runt — of the United Families of Earth, having failed to conquer Kayoss, (not even given control of the assault-bots!), doomed to spend his life fiddling with useless work, reduced to barely surviving on his Darsen Family retainer, with one, always just <u>one</u> wife, *who obviously doesn't enjoy sex with me. . . . My friends falling away as they become more successful, until my only companions become younger and younger men. . . .* Always playing baseball or basketball, <u>*not*</u> to cheering crowds, with no giant alien-insect Ttiiffsts to rescue and look after. . . . To never taste hkkkΩttt again. . . . *As long as I choose to live. . . .*

Whatever. . . .

◆

AFTERWARD

This is my second book published by iUniverse. Once again I have to thank the competence and the compassion of the consultants I worked with on _The Invasion of Peasant-Earth_ (Book-1) and _The Milky Galaxy_ (Book-2): Mae Genson, Samantha Anderson, and Reed Samuel.

THE PUBLISHING PROCESS

Since it takes, I'm told, an average of twenty years, while continuously submitting one's manuscript over and over, to find a publisher to accept one's work; at the age of 77, I had to finally admit I did not have twenty years left.

So rather than spend money for postage and manuscript-printing, I decided to pay for "self"-publishing. After a long search, I settled on Gatekeeper Press, which did not work out.

Trolling through my own library at home, I came upon the novel of a friend of mine I hadn't read in years: _Rainbow Plantation Blues_ by Robert L. Sheeley. I had helped him edit it, and he had gotten it "self"-published by iUniverse Publishing. Then I remembered I had another friend who published a few novels with iUniverse.

So I went with iUniverse for my own "self"-publishing. My experience with them has been positive — I think the cover art is amazingly good! — but we mis-communicated a bit about the formatting of the interior of my first book with them, _The Invasion of Peasant Earth_, so that I am not completely happy with it. Being a new customer, I did not understand their procedures.

I will be publishing six more novels with iUniverse — should I live long enough! — and I look forward to the interior formatting being more to my liking.

Barbara G Louise
Cleveland Heights, Ohio
summer, 2021
(suffering in the heat of Climate Change)

photo by Susan R. Schnur

in addition to *The Milky Galaxy*
AROUND THE MULTIVERSE. . . .
Cleaveland and the universe of this novel can be found somewhere in the infinite reaches of the *Multiverse,* along with: Utopia; Erewhon; Oz; Lilliput; Precipice CA; Shora; Le Guin's planets: Earthsea, Hain, Gethen, Annares, Forest, Aka; Heinlein's planets: his alternates of Mars and Venus, Luna Free State, New Beginnings, Secundus, Tertius, Blessed, Landfall, the Nine Worlds; the alternate-Mars of various SF authors: Barsoom, Malacandra, Salvay; the worlds of Barbara G Louise: Zomia, Kkhadee, Kayoss, Dyson Prime, Nueva Cuba; and so many other SF planets and places: Middle Earth, the Shire; Anthea, Kendra-on-the-Delta, Arun, Barrayar, Quaddiespace, Lucifer (the planet), Darkover, the Stand on Zanzibar, (the disk of) Gaia (in orbit of Saturn), Beninia, Mouth-of-Mattapoisett MA, the Golden Globe, Babylon 5, as well as the Star Trek and the Star Wars Galaxies.

Printed in the United States
by Baker & Taylor Publisher Services